JAMES KOCHALKA

THE GLORKIAN WARRIOR EATS ADVENTURE PIE

:01
First Second
New York

FOR ELI & OLIVER
AND DECLAN & MARIPOSA!
(YOU CAN HEAR THEIR VOICES IN THE
GLORKIAN WARRIOR VIDEO GAME.)

VISIT GLORKIANWARRIOR.COM

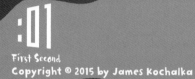

:01
First Second
Copyright © 2015 by James Kochalka

Published by First Second
First Second is an imprint of Roaring Brook Press,
a division of Holtzbrinck Publishing Holdings Limited Partnership
175 Fifth Avenue, New York, New York 10010
All rights reserved

"Attract Mode" originally appeared in *The Devastator* №4

Cataloging-in-Publication Data is on file at the Library of Congress.

Paperback ISBN 978-1-62672-021-3
Hardcover ISBN 978-1-62672-133-3

First Second books may be purchased for business or promotional use. For information
on bulk purchases please contact Macmillan Corporate and Premium Sales
Department at (800) 221-7945 x5442 or by email at specialmarkets@macmillan.com.

First edition 2015
Book design by Colleen AF Venable

Printed in China by Macmillan Production (Asia) Ltd.,
Kowloon Bay, Hong Kong (supplier code 10)

Paperback: 10 9 8 7 6 5 4 3 2 1
Hardcover: 10 9 8 7 6 5 4 3 2 1

J-GN
GLORKIAN
WARRIOR
436-9529

CHAPTER ONE

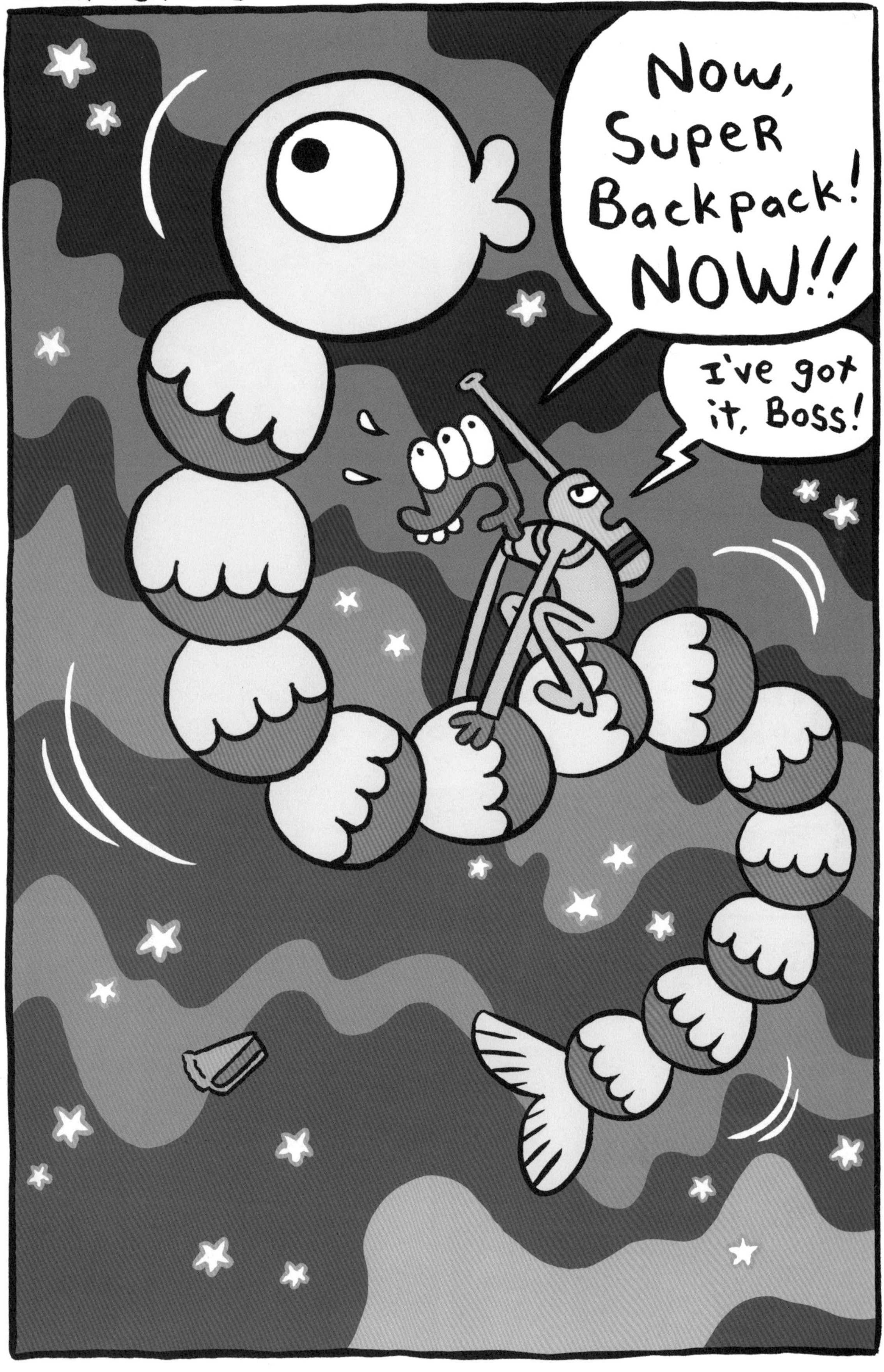
Now, Super Backpack! NOW!!
I've got it, Boss!

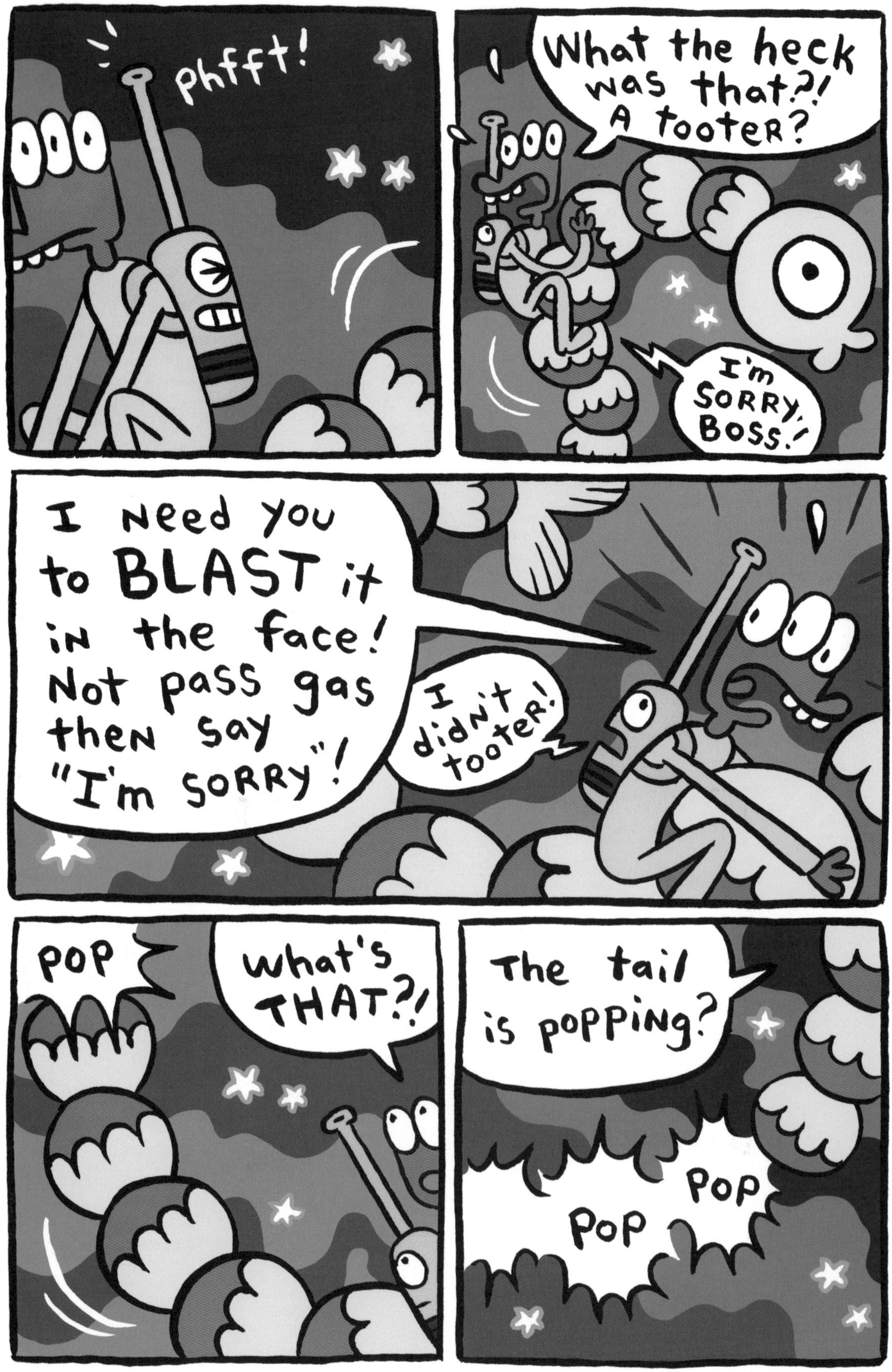
phfft!
What the heck was that?! A tooter?
I'm SORRY, BOSS!
I need you to BLAST it in the face! Not pass gas then say "I'm SORRY"!
I didn't tooter!
POP
What's THAT?!
The tail is popping?
POP
POP

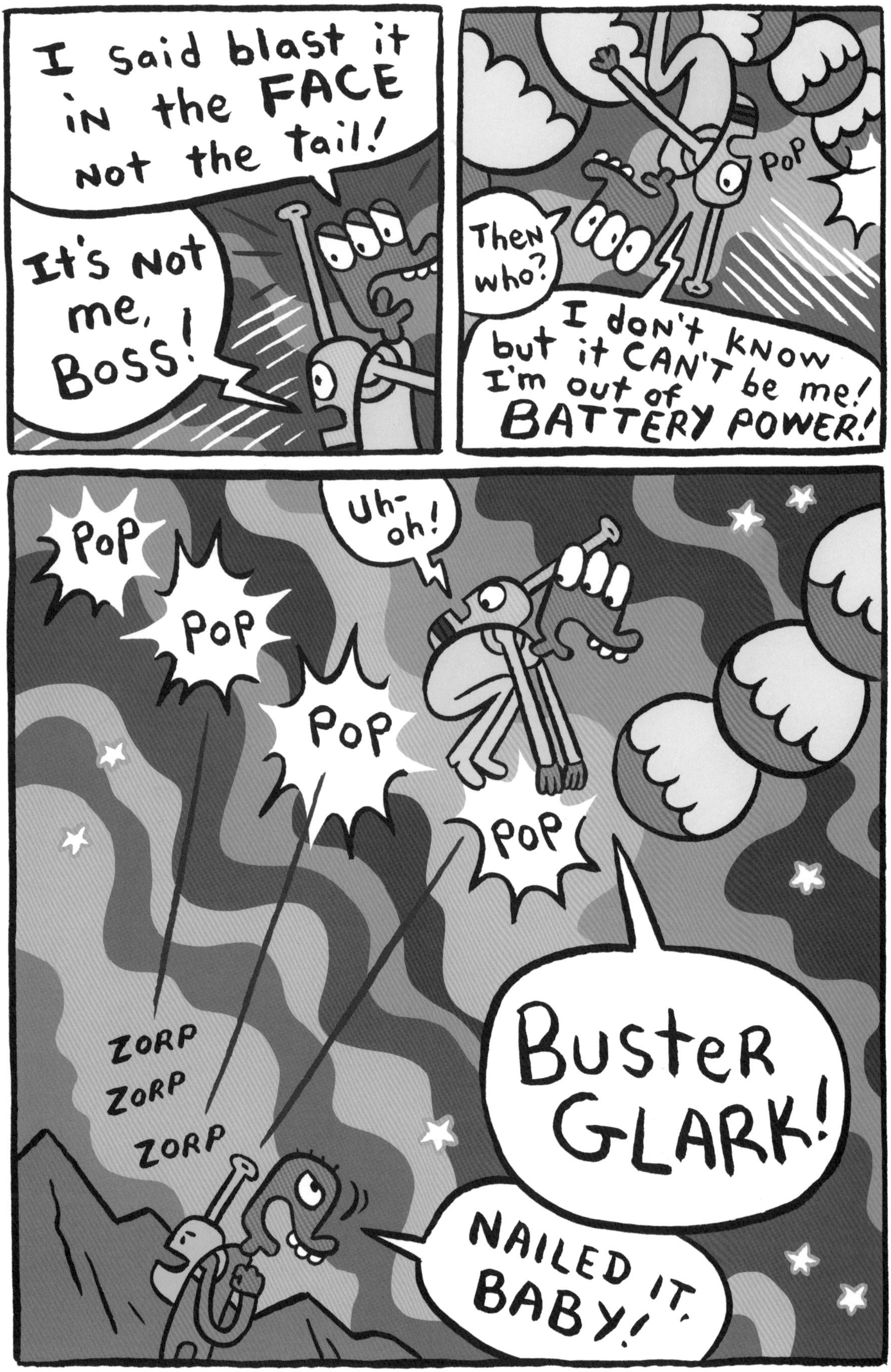

I said blast it in the FACE not the tail!
It's not me, Boss!
POP
Then who?
I don't know but it CAN'T be me! I'm out of BATTERY POWER!
POP
POP
POP
Uh-oh!
POP
ZORP
ZORP
ZORP
Buster GLARK!
NAILED IT, BABY!

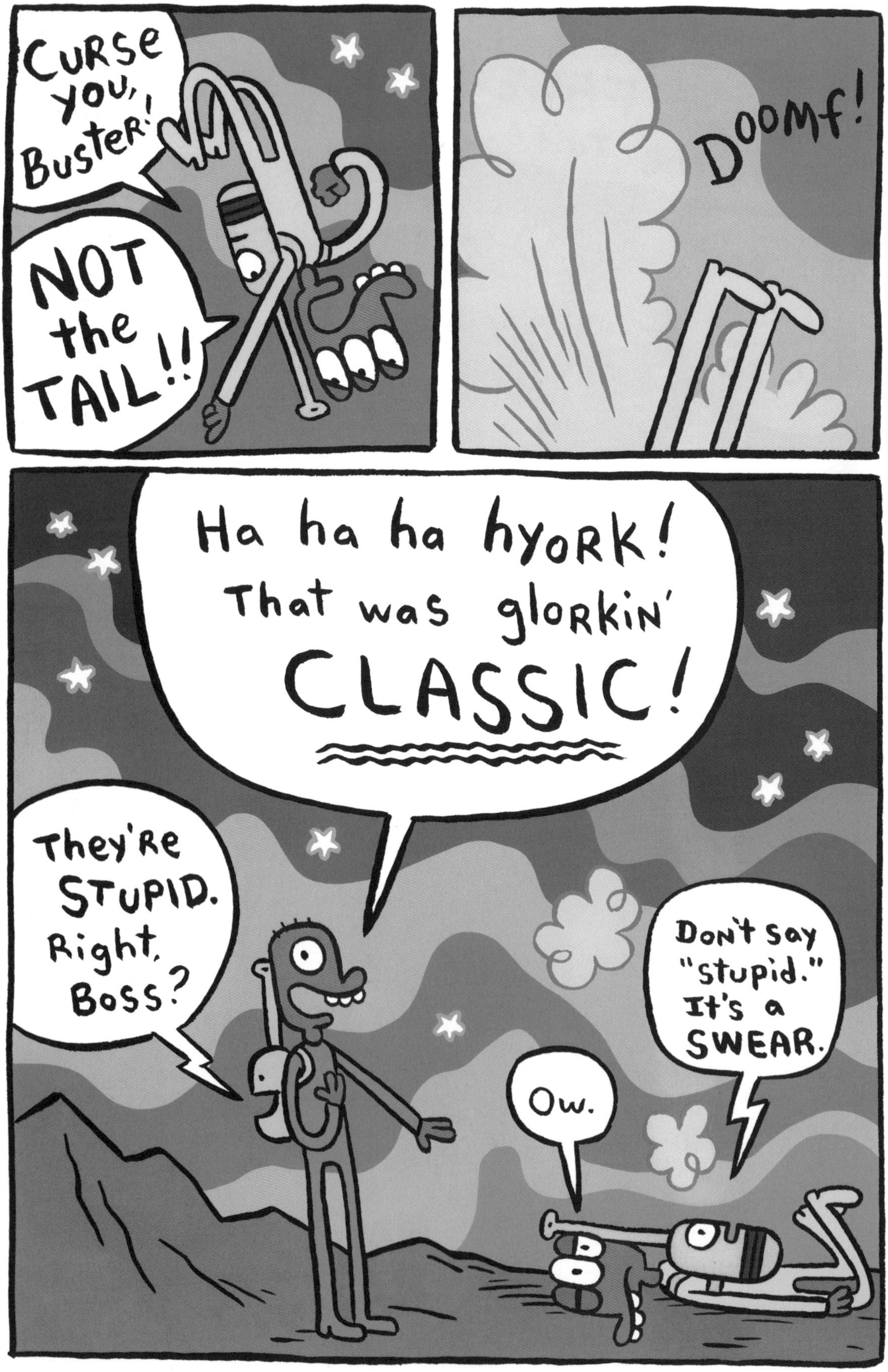
CURSE YOU, BUSTER!
NOT the TAIL!!
DOOMF!
Ha ha ha hyORK! That was glorkin' CLASSIC!
They're STUPID. Right, Boss?
Ow.
Don't say "stupid." It's a SWEAR.

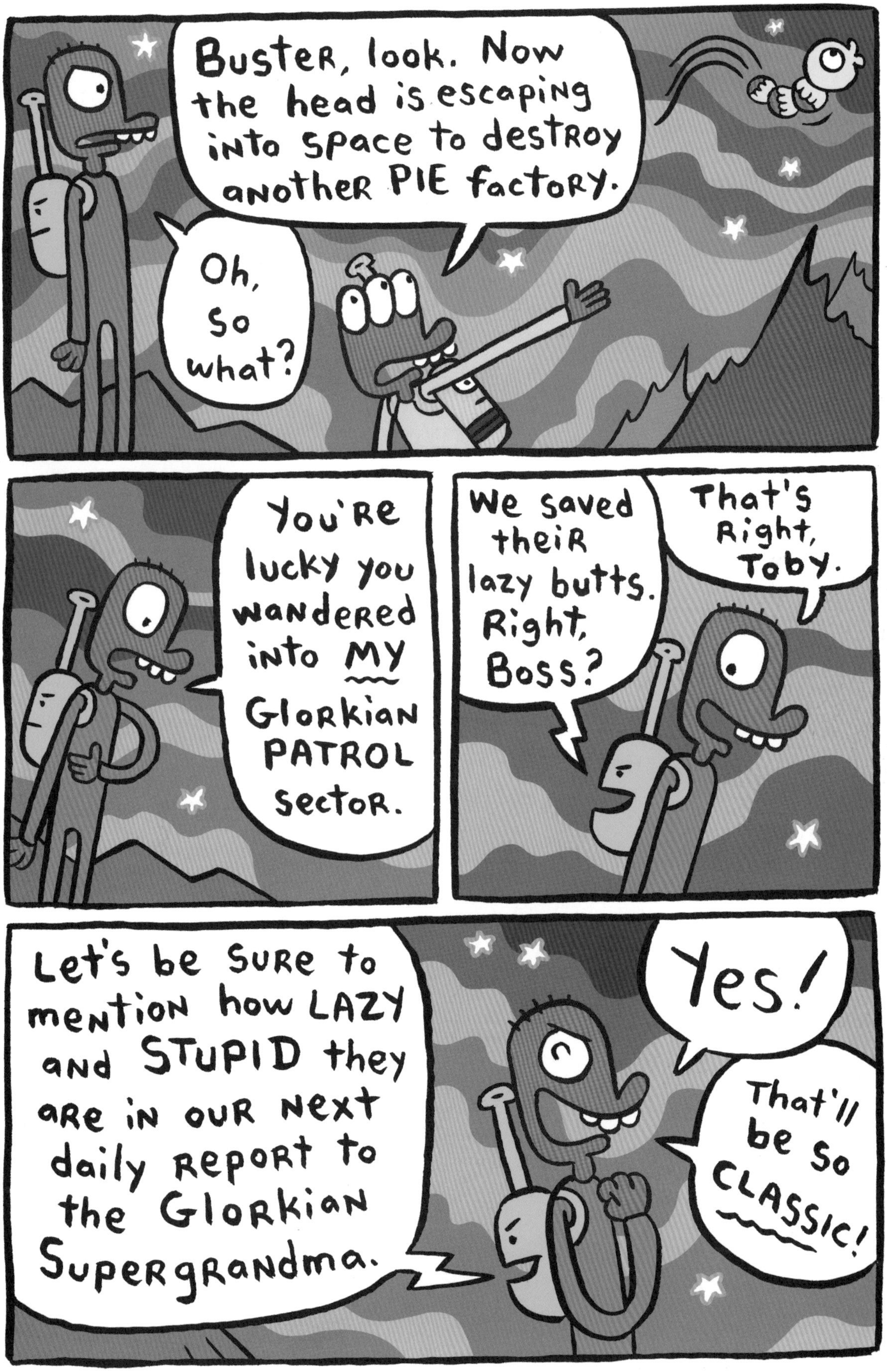

Buster, look. Now the head is escaping into space to destroy another PIE factory.
Oh, so what?
You're lucky you wandered into MY Glorkian PATROL sector.
We saved their lazy butts. Right, Boss?
That's Right, Toby.
Let's be sure to mention how LAZY and STUPID they are in our next daily report to the Glorkian Supergrandma.
Yes!
That'll be so CLASSIC!

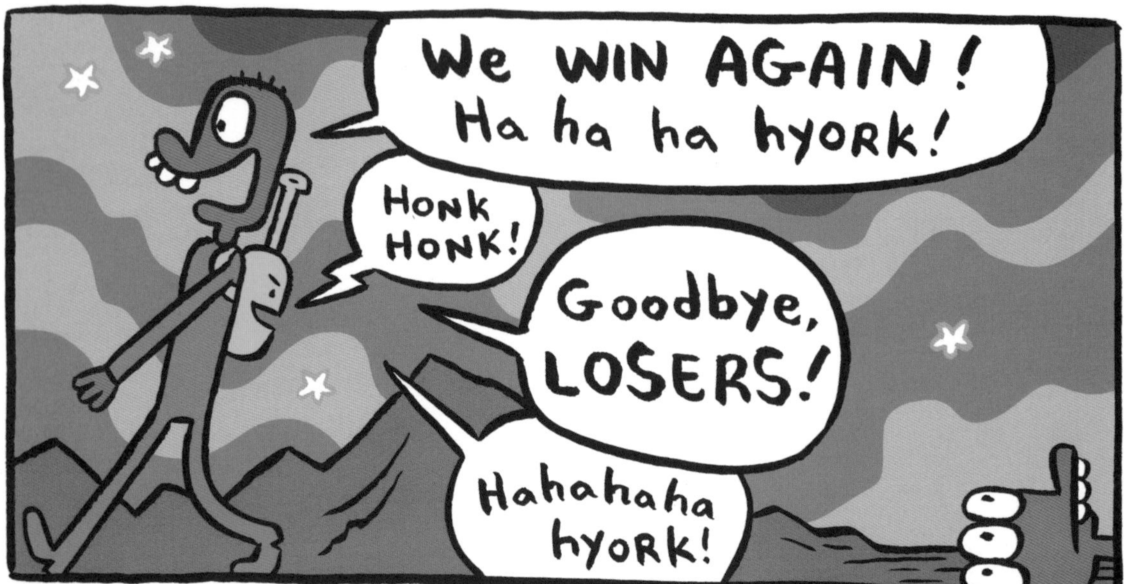
We WIN AGAIN! Ha ha ha hyork!
HONK HONK!
Goodbye, LOSERS!
Hahahaha hyork!

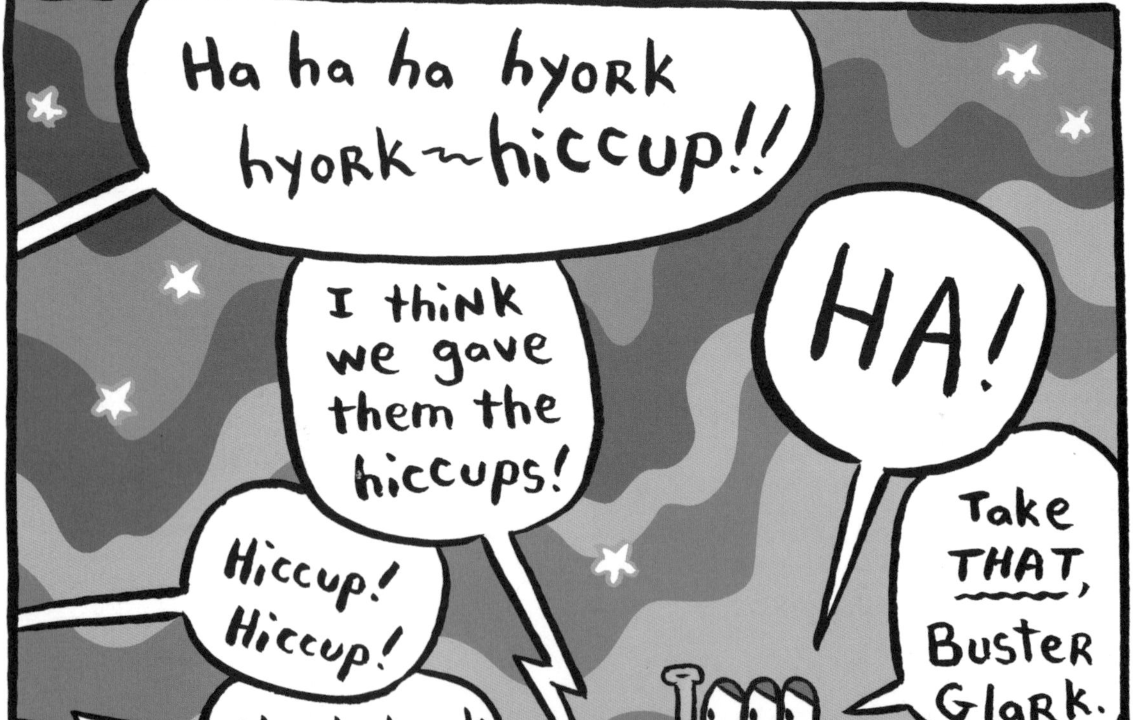
Ha ha ha hyork hyork~hiccup!!
I think we gave them the hiccups!
Hiccup! Hiccup!
HONK honk ~HONKup!
HA!
Take THAT, Buster Glark.
WE win!

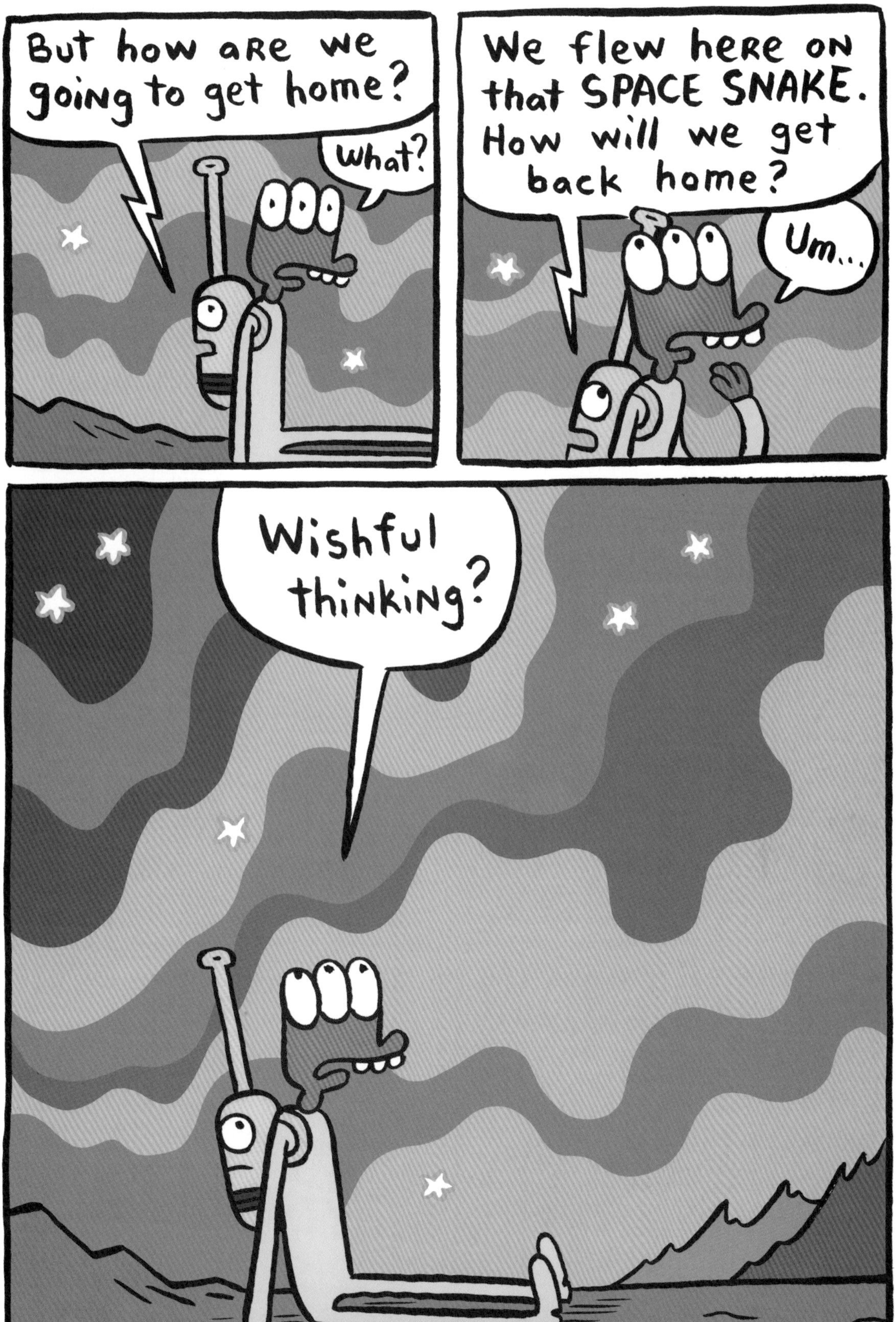
But how are we going to get home?
What?
We flew here on that SPACE SNAKE. How will we get back home?
Um...
Wishful thinking?

CHAPTER TWO

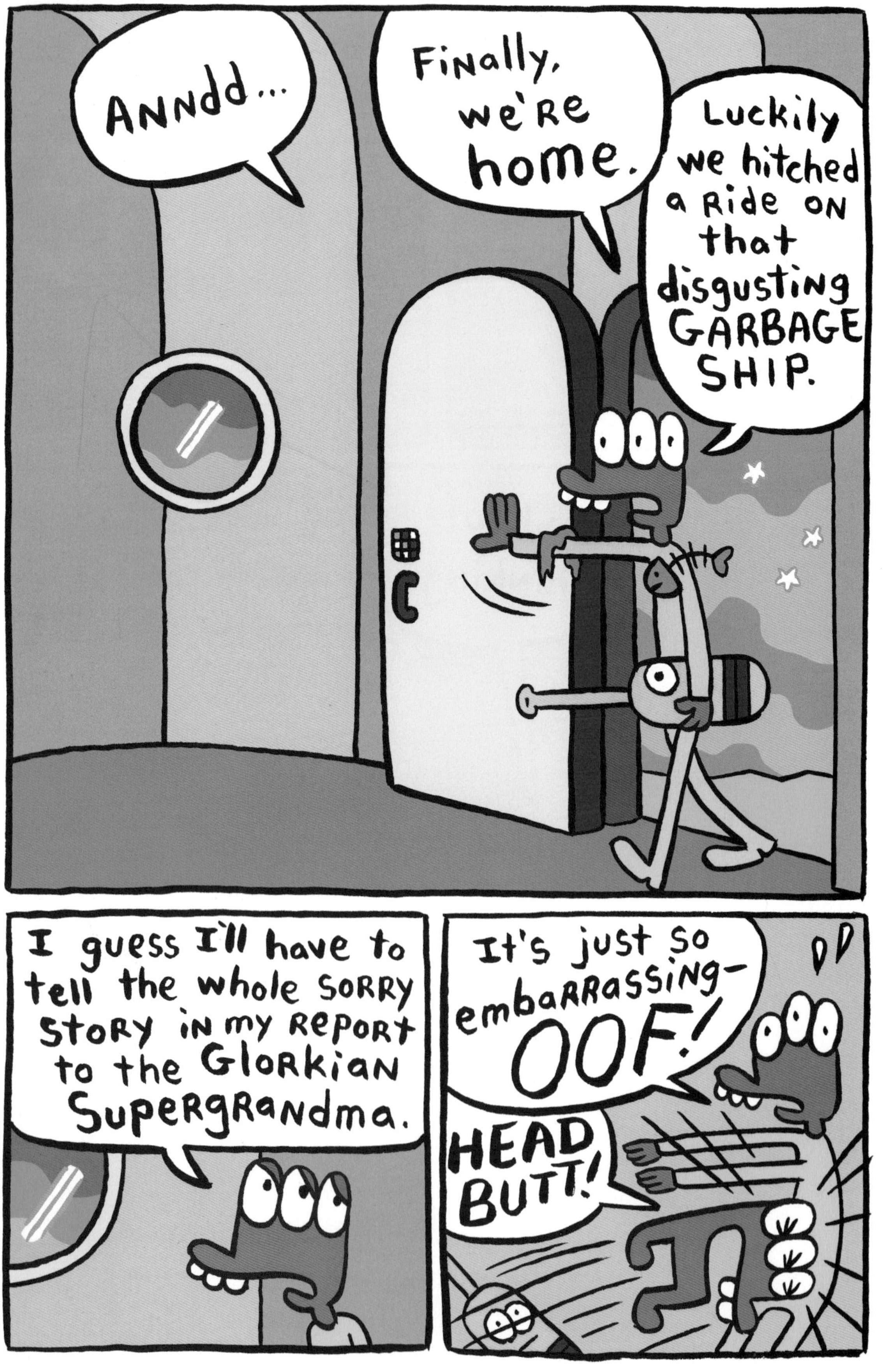
ANNdd...
Finally, we're home.
Luckily we hitched a ride on that disgusting GARBAGE SHIP.
I guess I'll have to tell the whole SORRY story in my report to the Glorkian Supergrandma.
It's just so embarrassing- OOF!
HEAD BUTT!

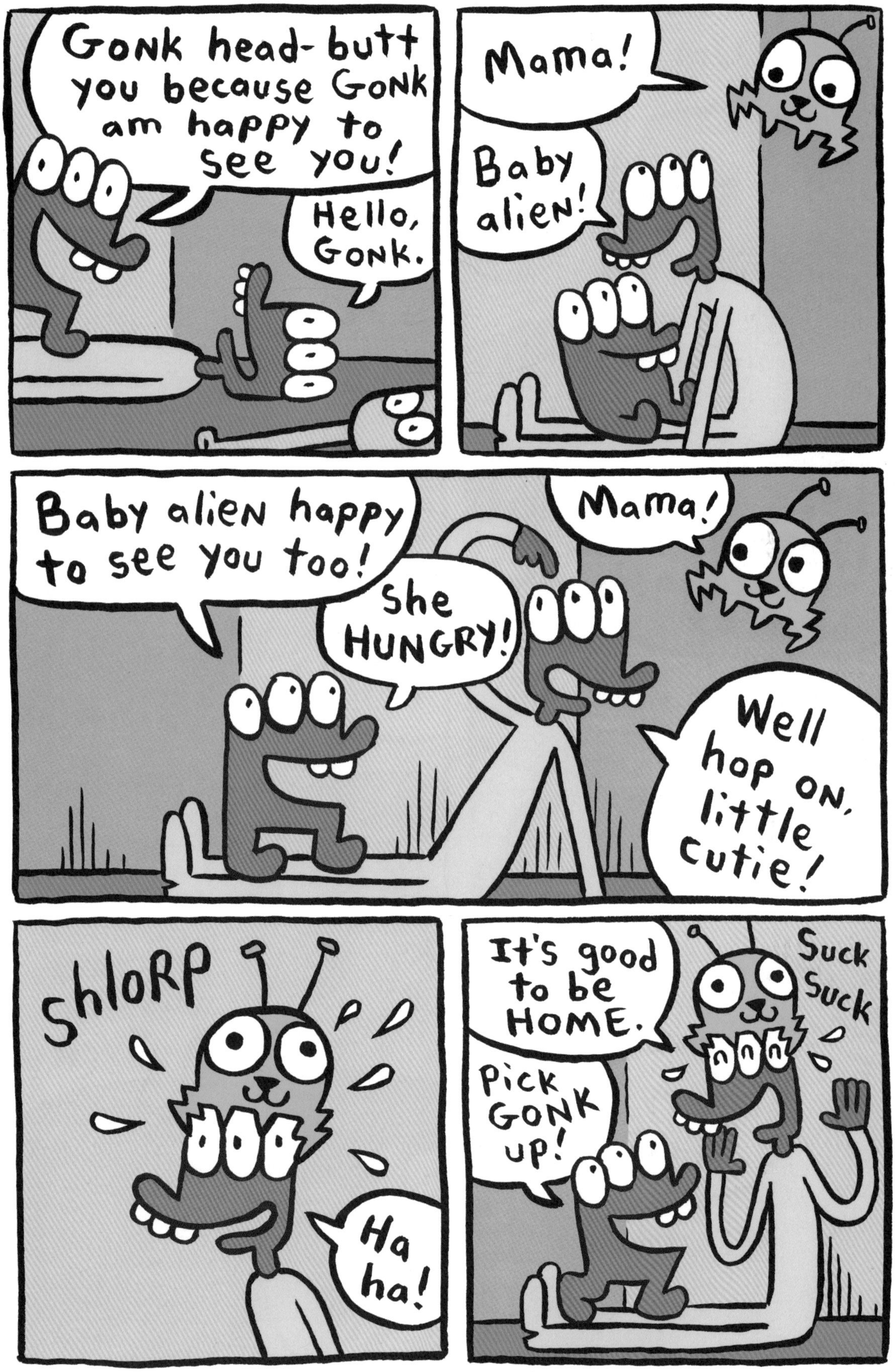
Gonk head-butt you because Gonk am happy to see you!
Hello, Gonk.
Mama!
Baby alien!
Baby alien happy to see you too!
She HUNGRY!
Mama!
Well hop on, little cutie!
Shlorp
Ha ha!
It's good to be HOME.
Suck Suck
Pick GONK up!

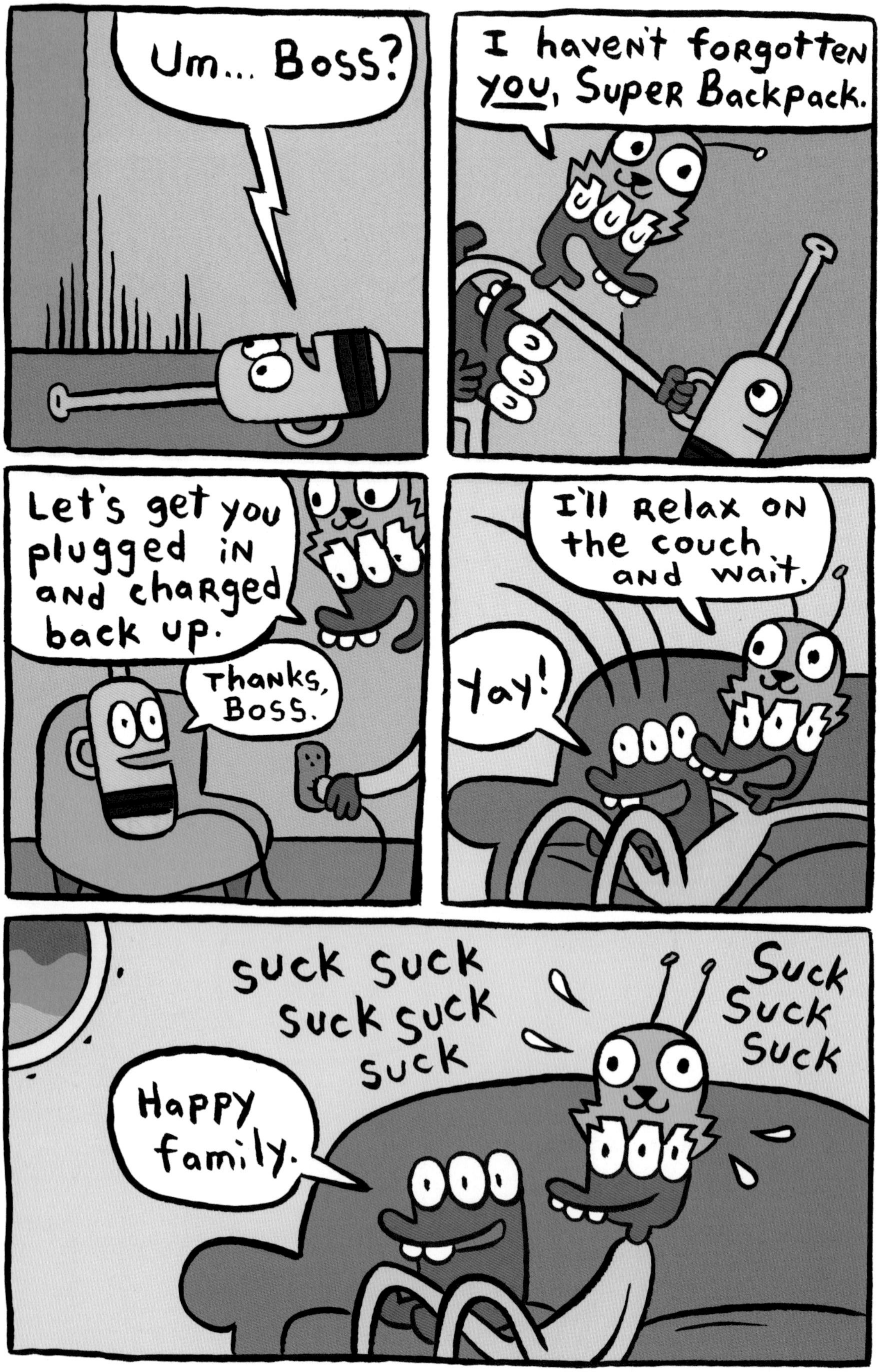
Um... Boss?
I haven't forgotten YOU, Super Backpack.
Let's get you plugged in and charged back up.
Thanks, Boss.
I'll relax on the couch and wait.
Yay!
suck suck suck suck suck
Suck Suck Suck
Happy family.

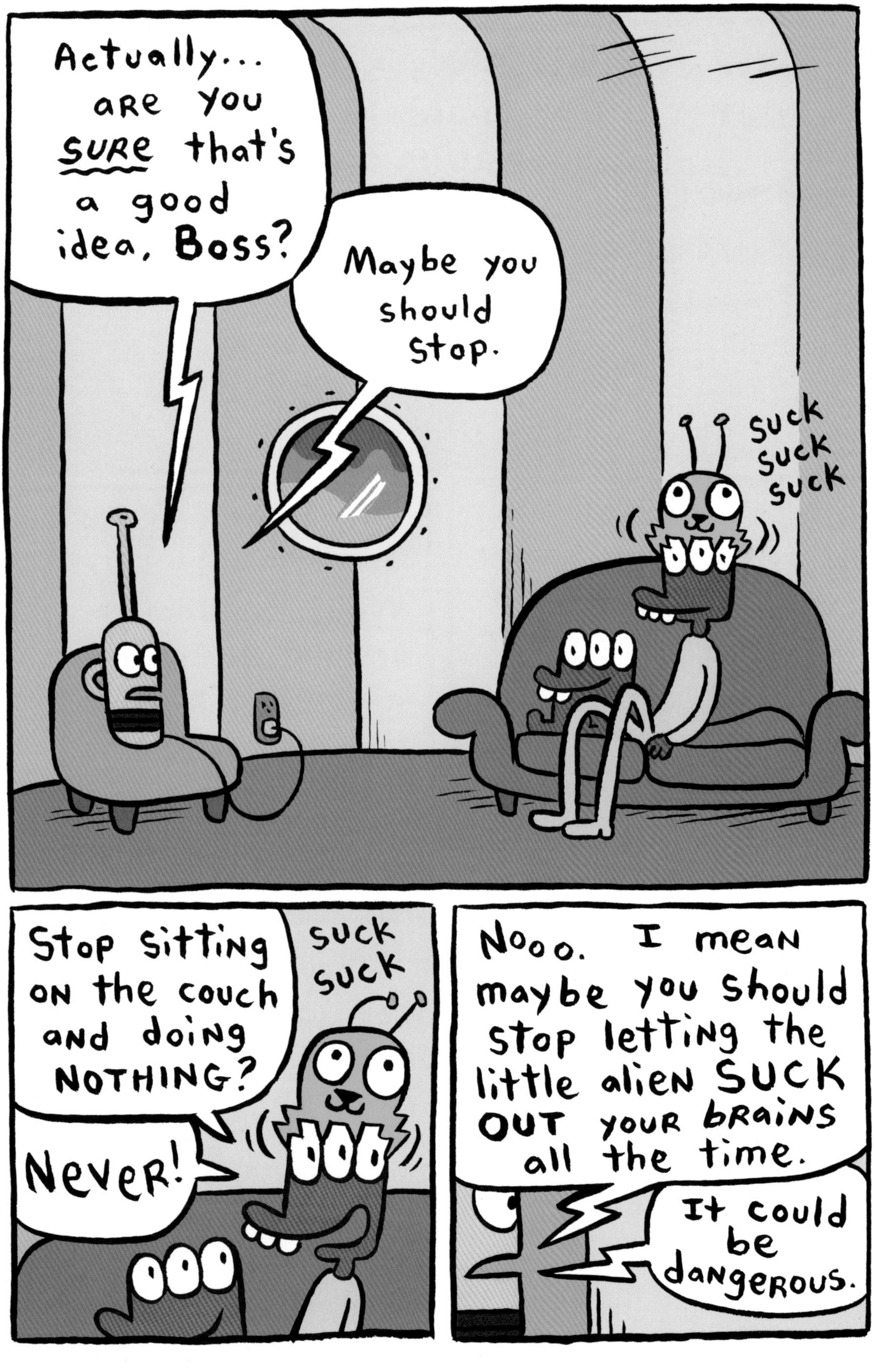
Actually... are you SURE that's a good idea, Boss?
Maybe you should stop.
suck suck suck
Stop sitting on the couch and doing NOTHING?
suck suck
Never!
Nooo. I mean maybe you should stop letting the little alien SUCK OUT your brains all the time.
It could be dangerous.

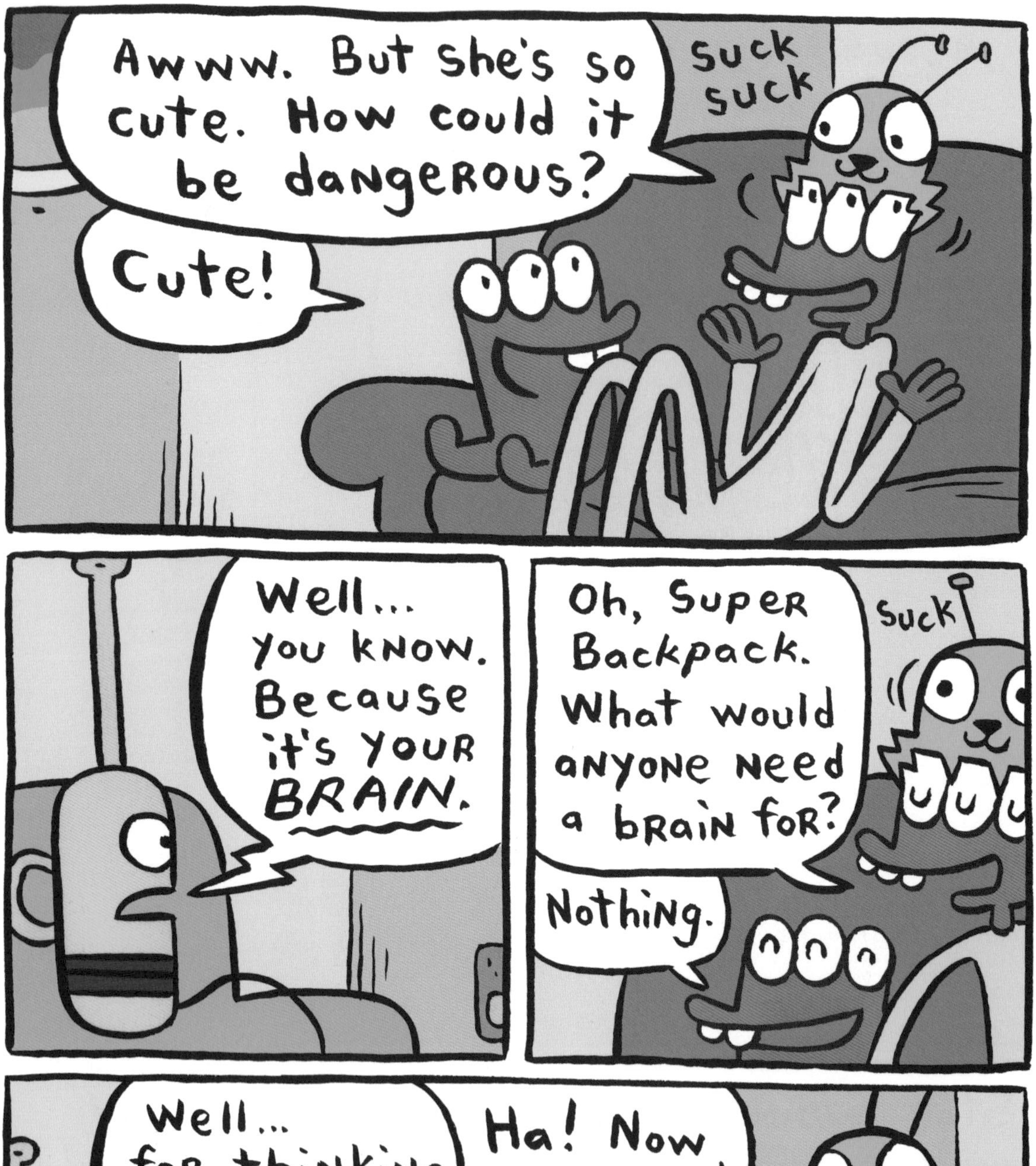
Awww. But she's so cute. How could it be dangerous?
Cute!
suck suck
Well... you know. Because it's your BRAIN.
Oh, Super Backpack. What would anyone need a brain for?
suck
Nothing.
Well... for thinking of stuff. Having ideas. Knowing things.
Ha! Now you're just being silly.
Silly.

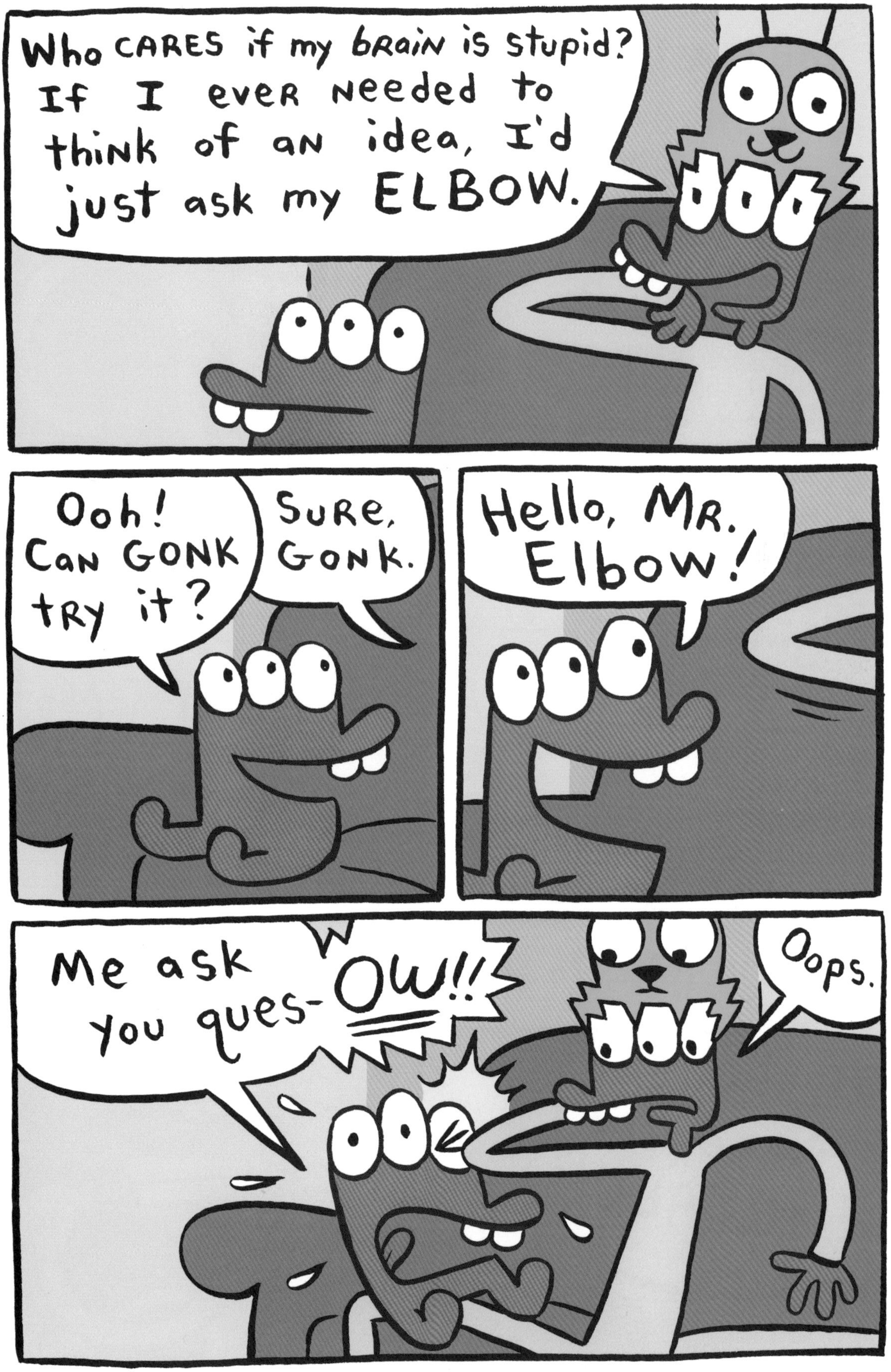
Who CARES if my brain is stupid? If I ever needed to think of an idea, I'd just ask my ELBOW.
Ooh! Can GONK try it?
Sure, Gonk.
Hello, Mr. Elbow!
Me ask you ques-
OW!!
Oops.

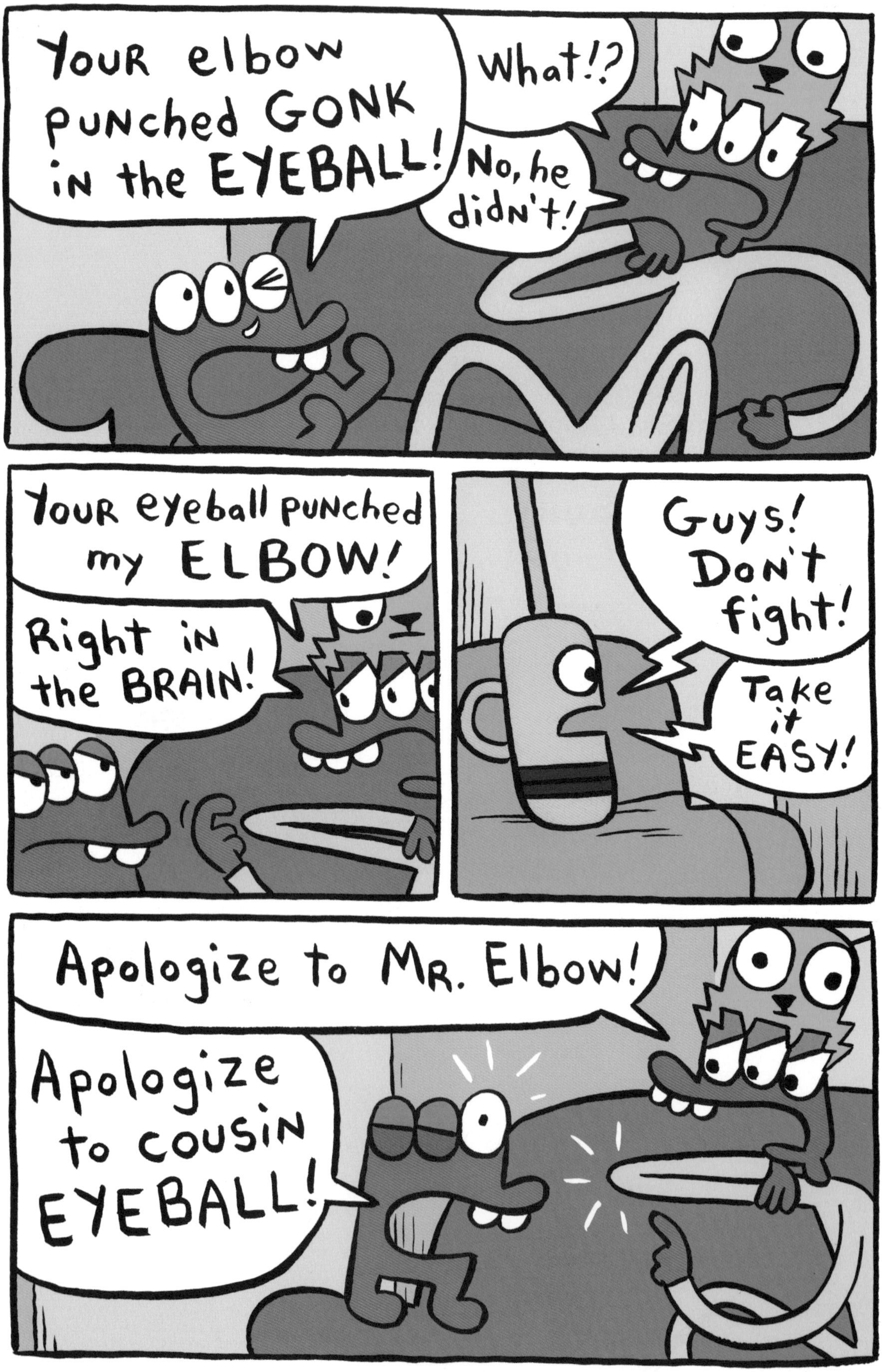
Your elbow punched GONK in the EYEBALL!
What!?
No, he didn't!
Your eyeball punched my ELBOW!
Right in the BRAIN!
Guys! Don't fight!
Take it EASY!
Apologize to Mr. Elbow!
Apologize to cousin EYEBALL!

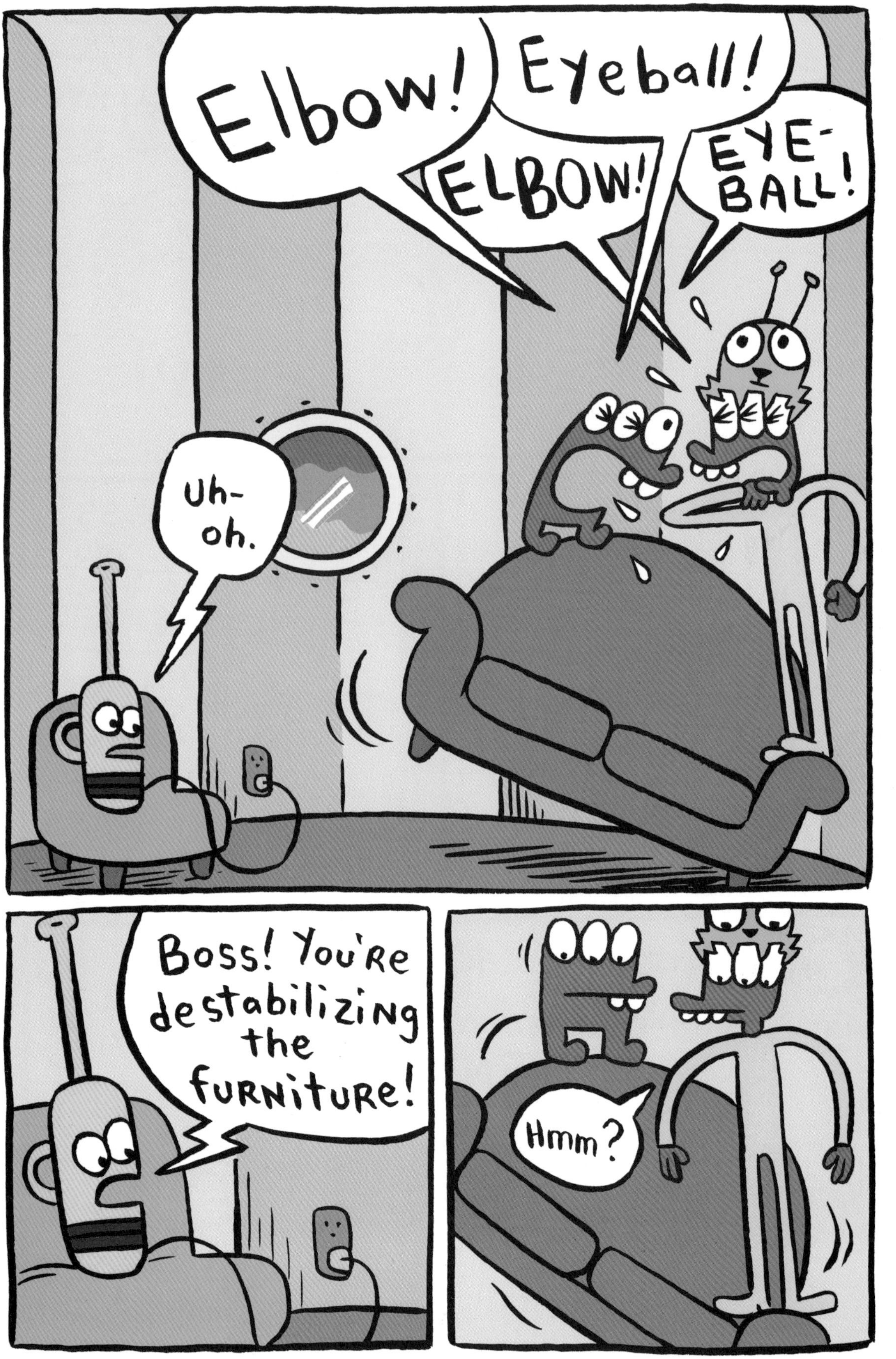
Elbow!
Eyeball!
ELBOW!
EYE-BALL!
Uh-oh.
Boss! You're destabilizing the furniture!
Hmm?

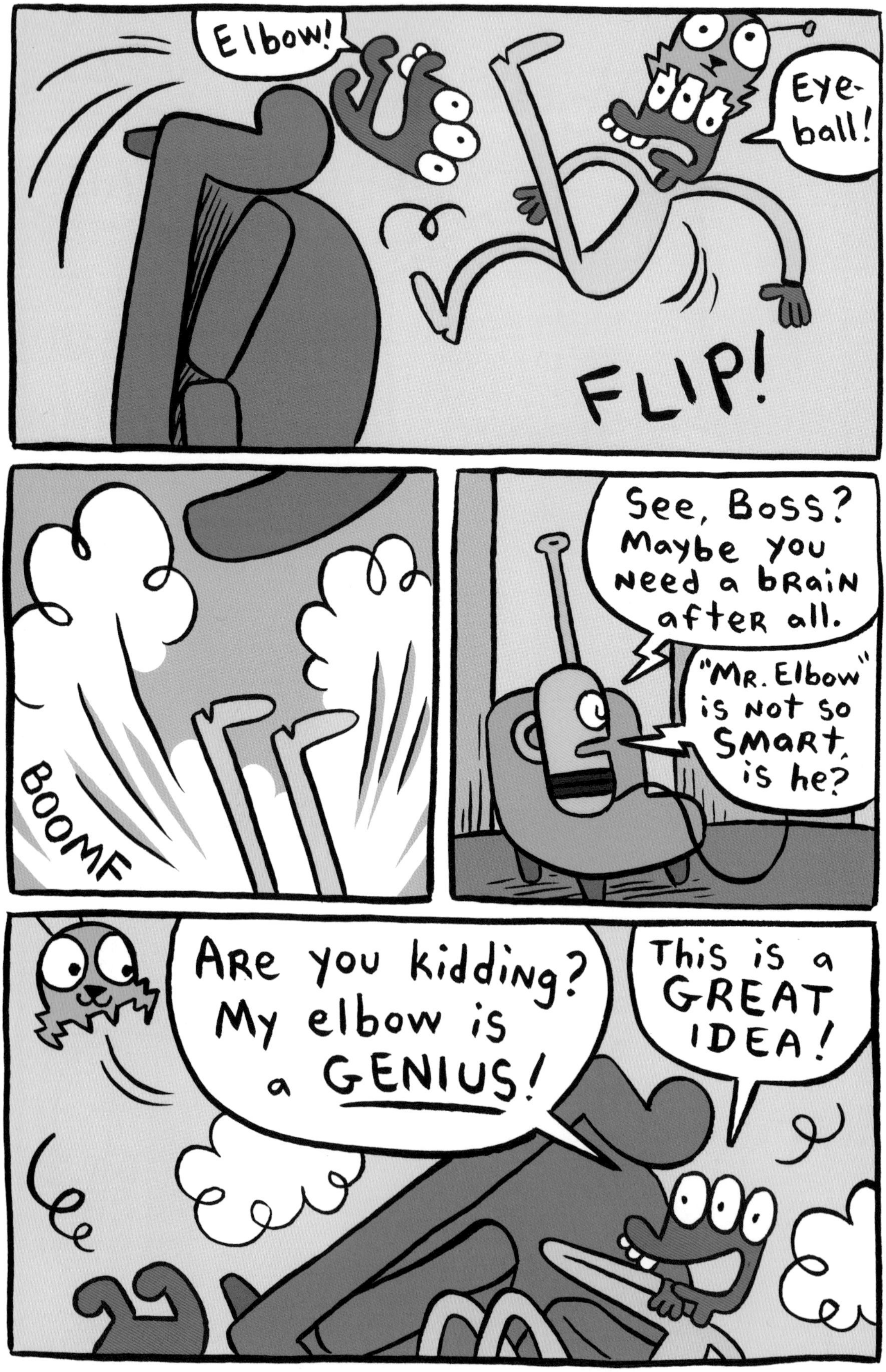
Elbow!
Eye-ball!
FLIP!
BOOMF
See, Boss? Maybe you need a brain after all.
"Mr. Elbow" is not so smart, is he?
Are you kidding? My elbow is a GENIUS!
This is a GREAT IDEA!

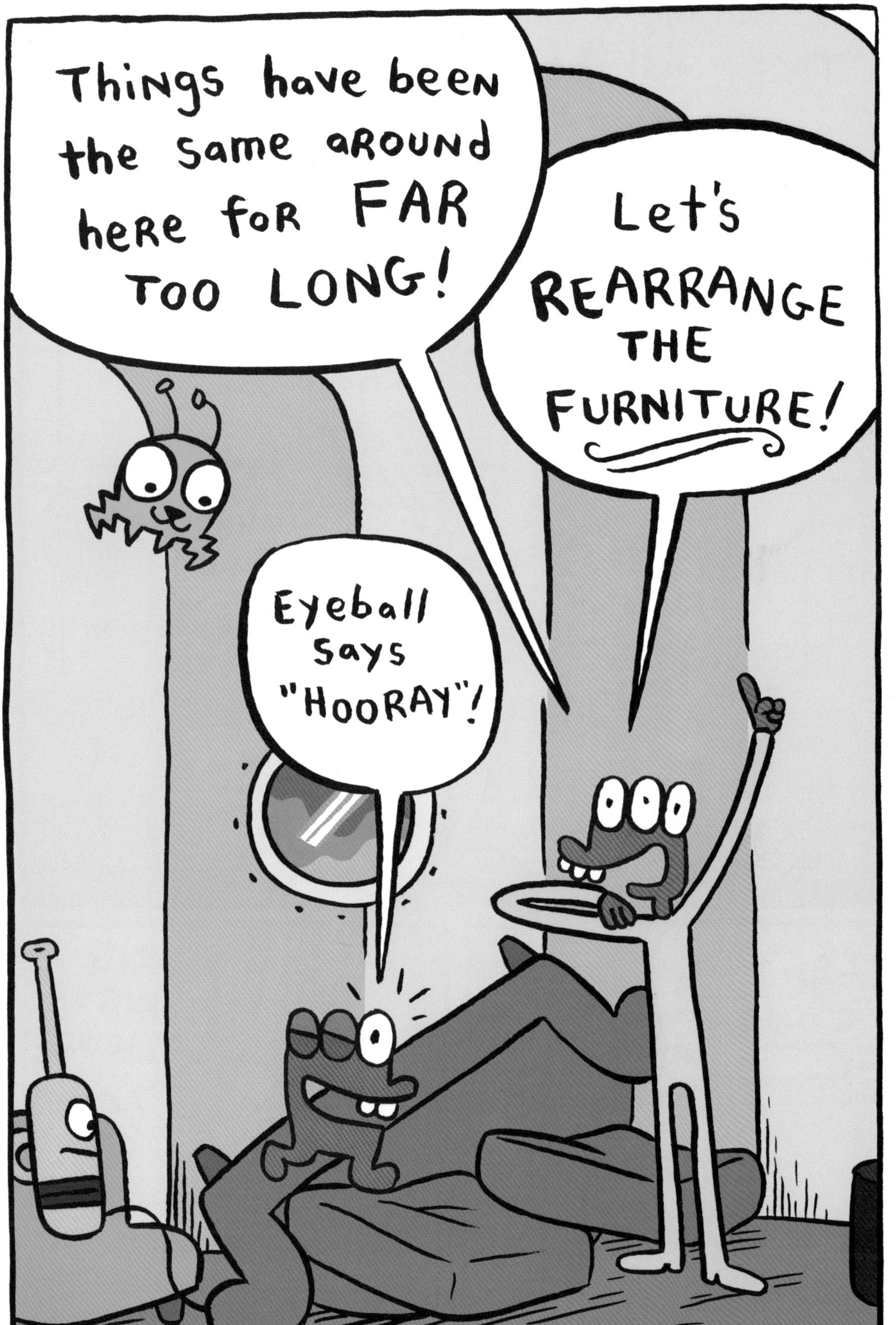
Things have been the same around here for FAR TOO LONG!
Let's REARRANGE THE FURNITURE!
Eyeball says "HOORAY"!

CHAPTER THREE

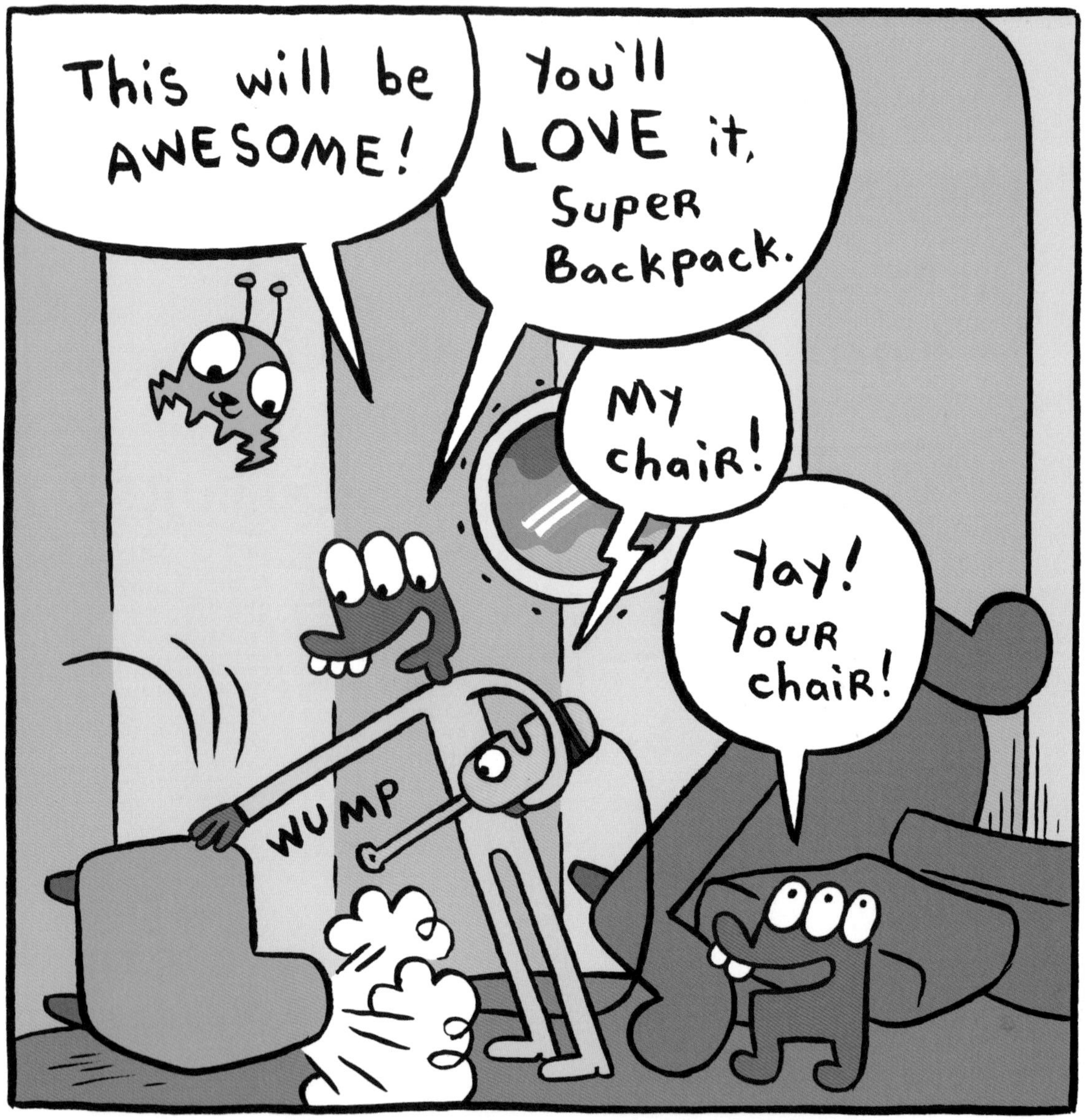
This will be AWESOME!
You'll LOVE it, Super Backpack.
My chair!
Yay! Your chair!
WUMP

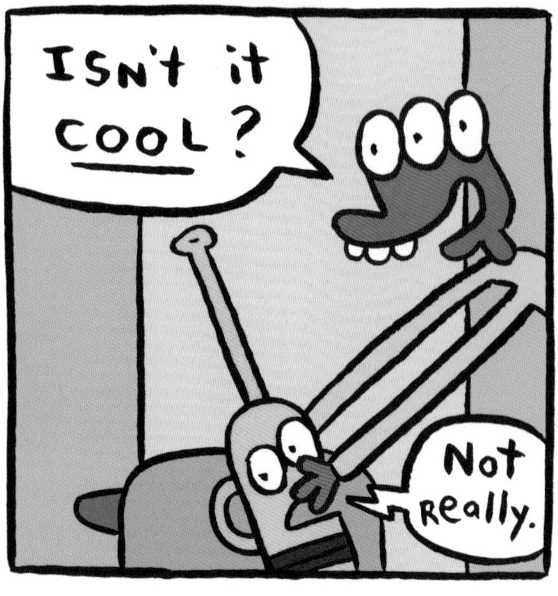
Isn't it COOL?
Not really.

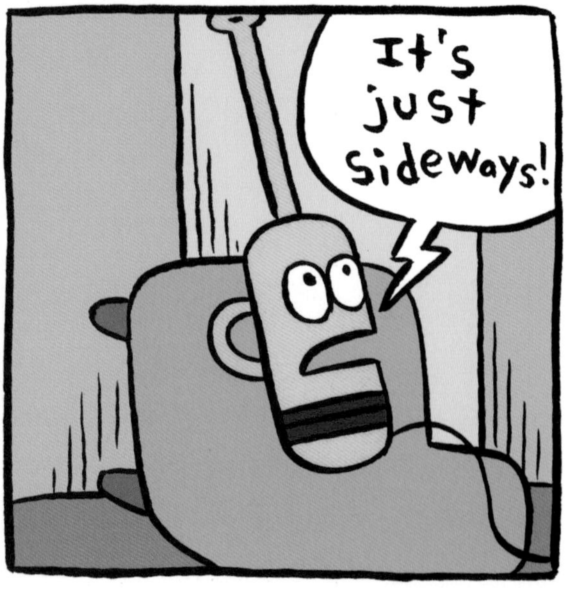
It's just sideways!

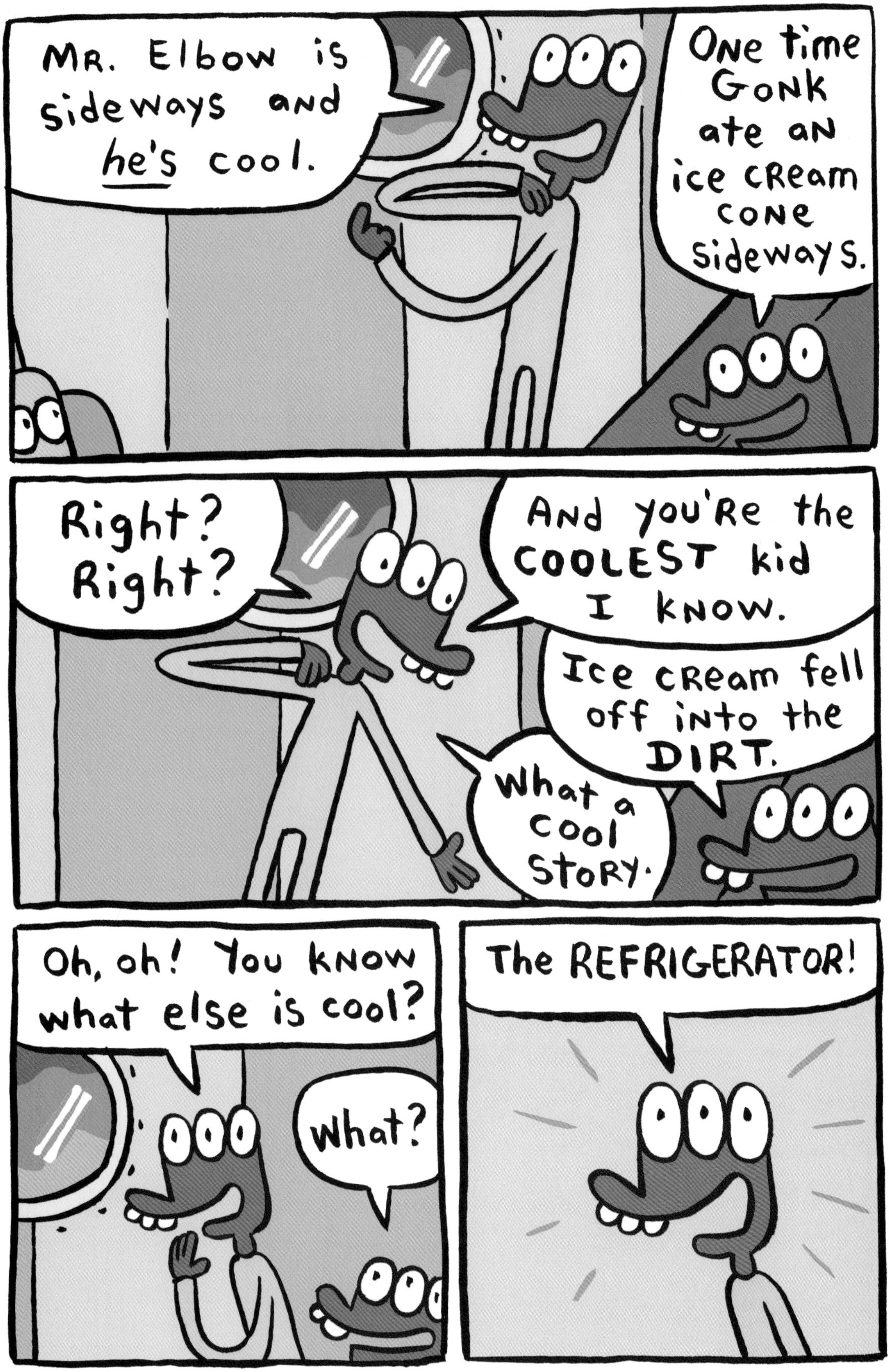
MR. Elbow is sideways and he's cool.
One time GONK ate an ice cream cone sideways.
Right? Right?
And you're the COOLEST kid I know.
Ice cream fell off into the DIRT.
What a cool story.
Oh, oh! You know what else is cool?
What?
The REFRIGERATOR!

Hey, hey, hey!
We could even put the hyper-fridge ON TOP of the couch!
Why?

Never ask your elbow "WHY?"
That would be Ridiculous!
Repicklemush.

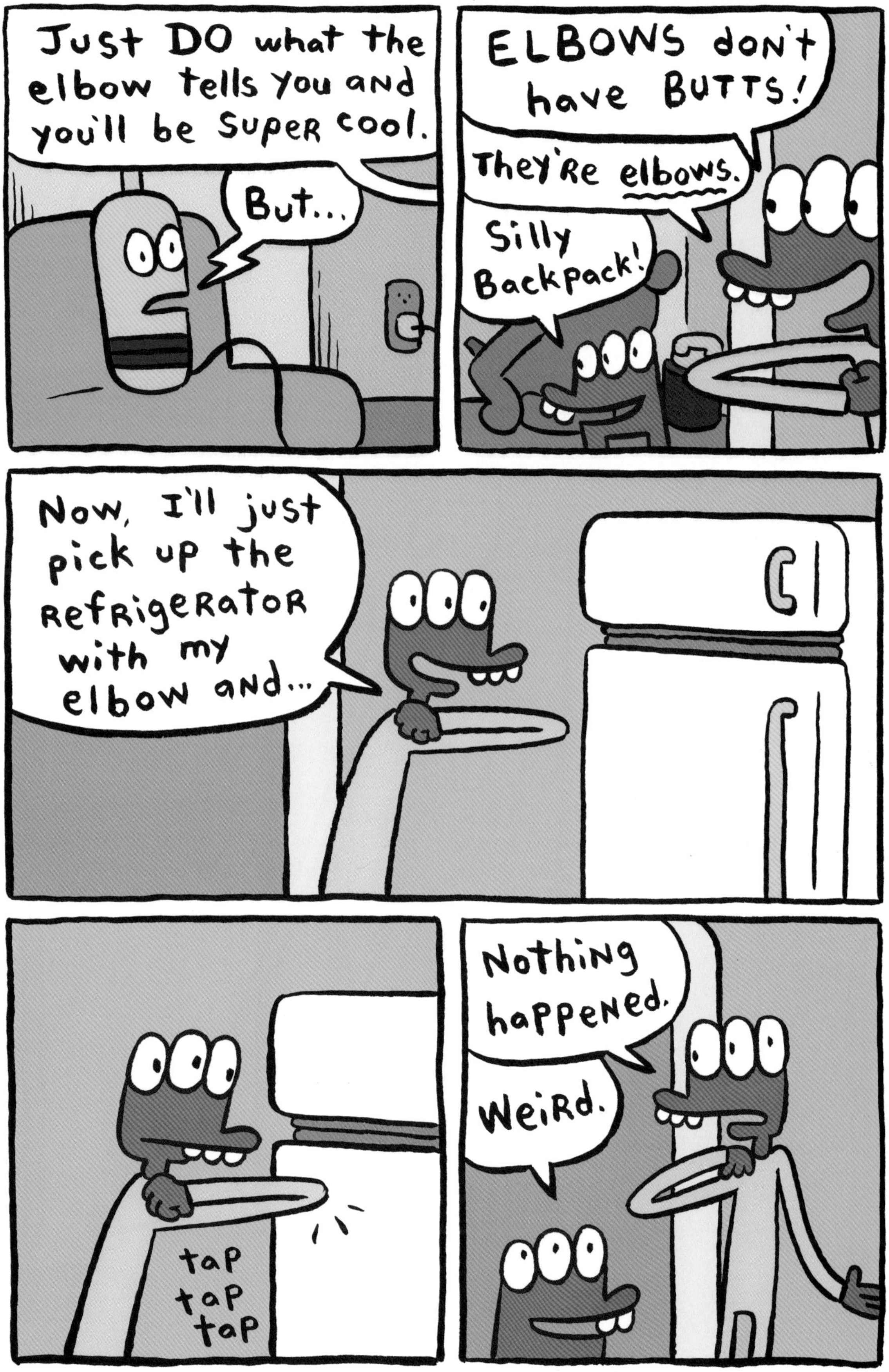
Just DO what the elbow tells you and you'll be super cool.
But...
ELBOWS don't have BUTTS!
They're elbows.
Silly Backpack!
Now, I'll just pick up the refrigerator with my elbow and...
tap tap tap
Nothing happened.
Weird.

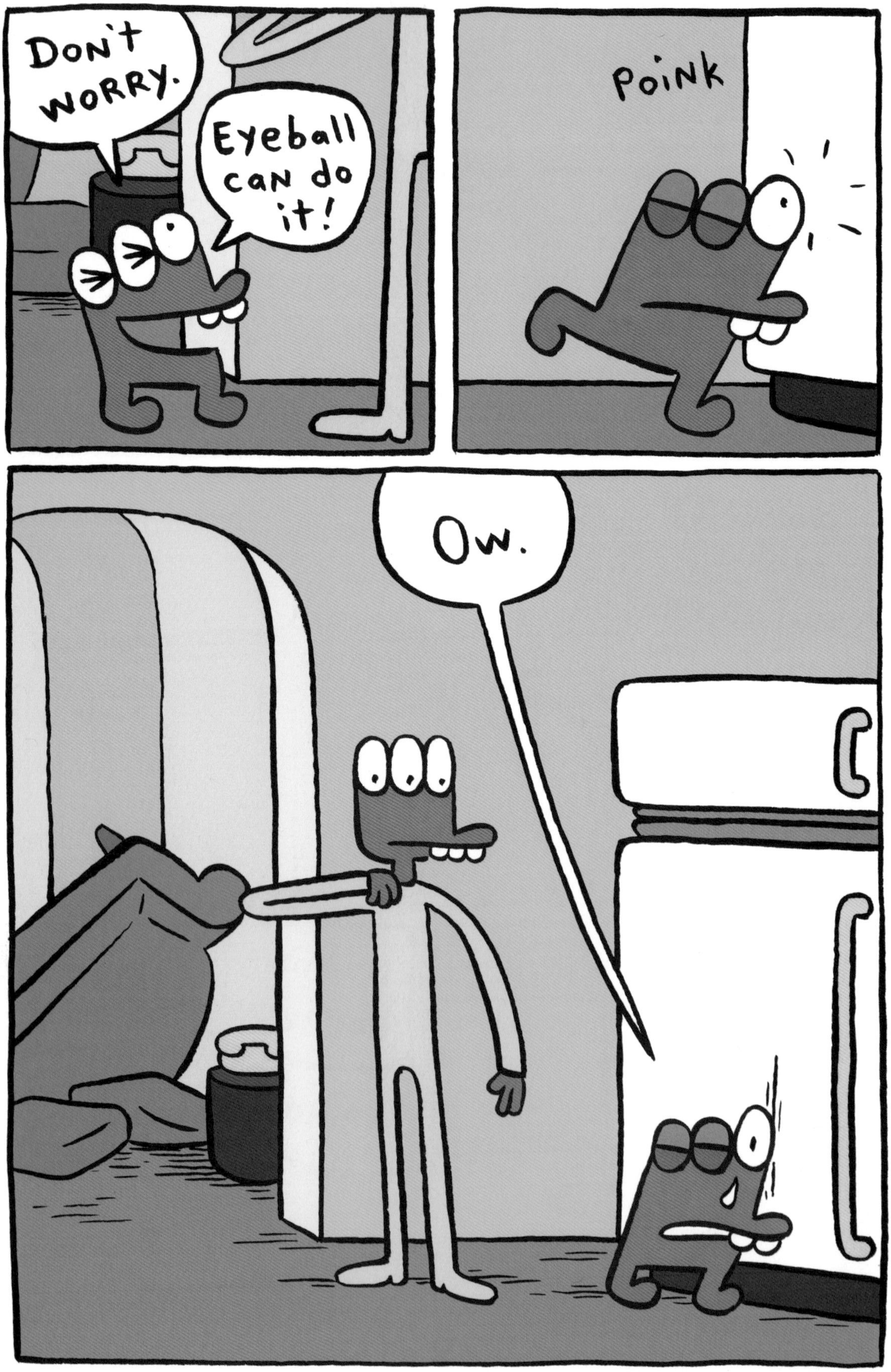
Don't worry.
Eyeball can do it!
POINK
Ow.

CHAPTER FOUR

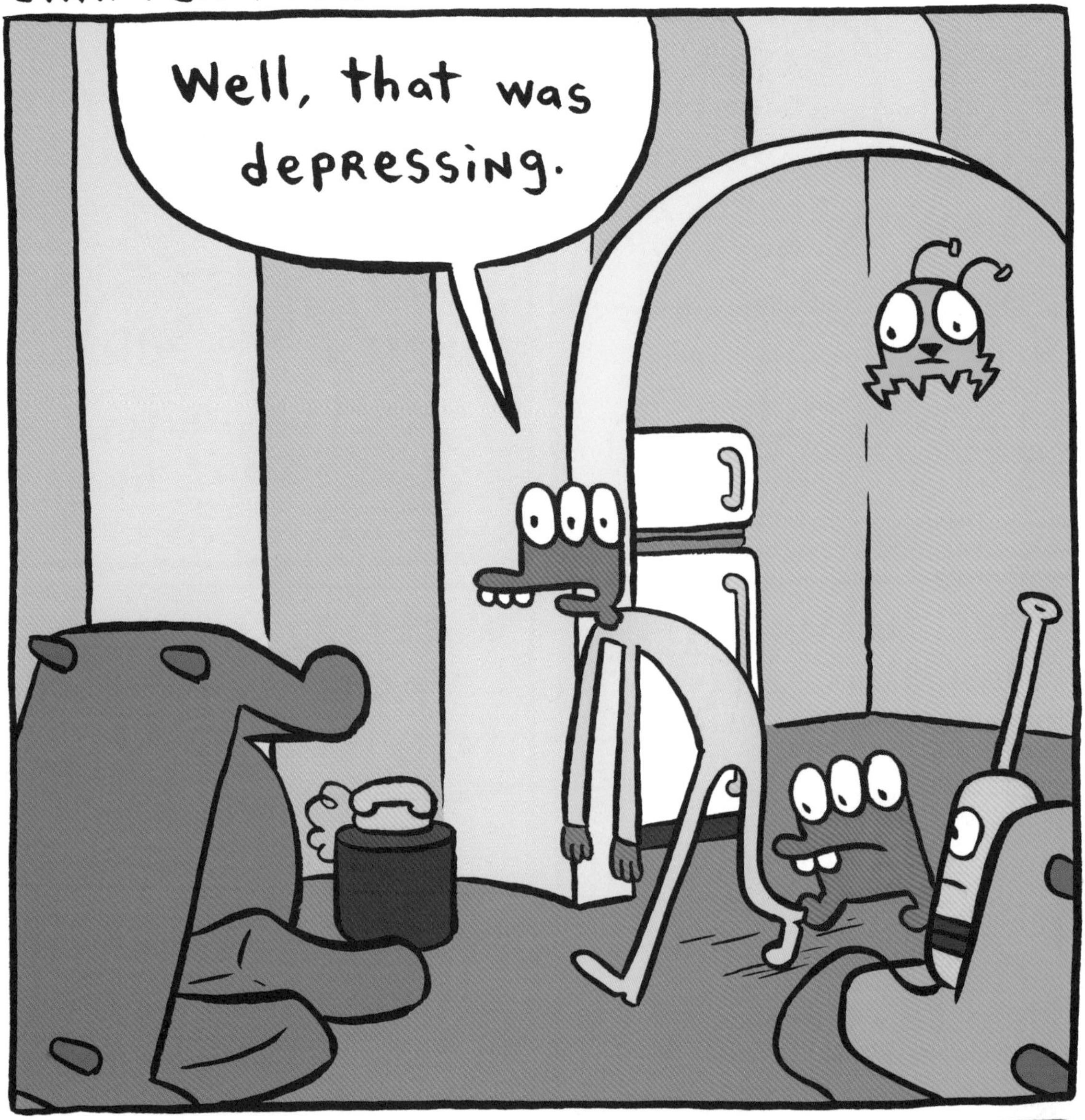
Well, that was depressing.

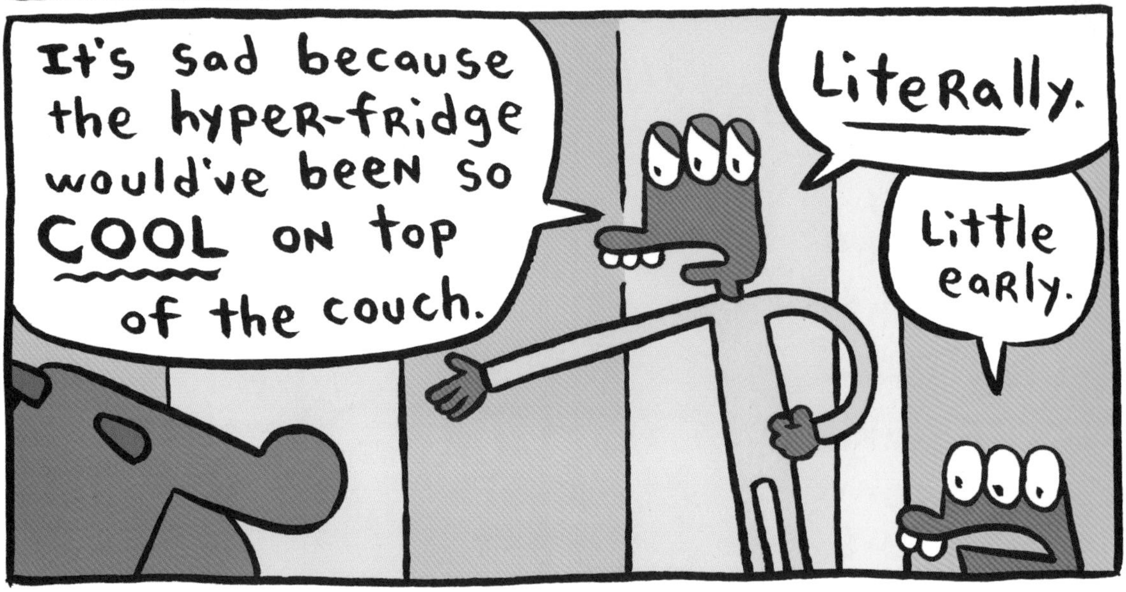
It's sad because the hyper-fridge would've been so COOL on top of the couch.
Literally.
Little early.

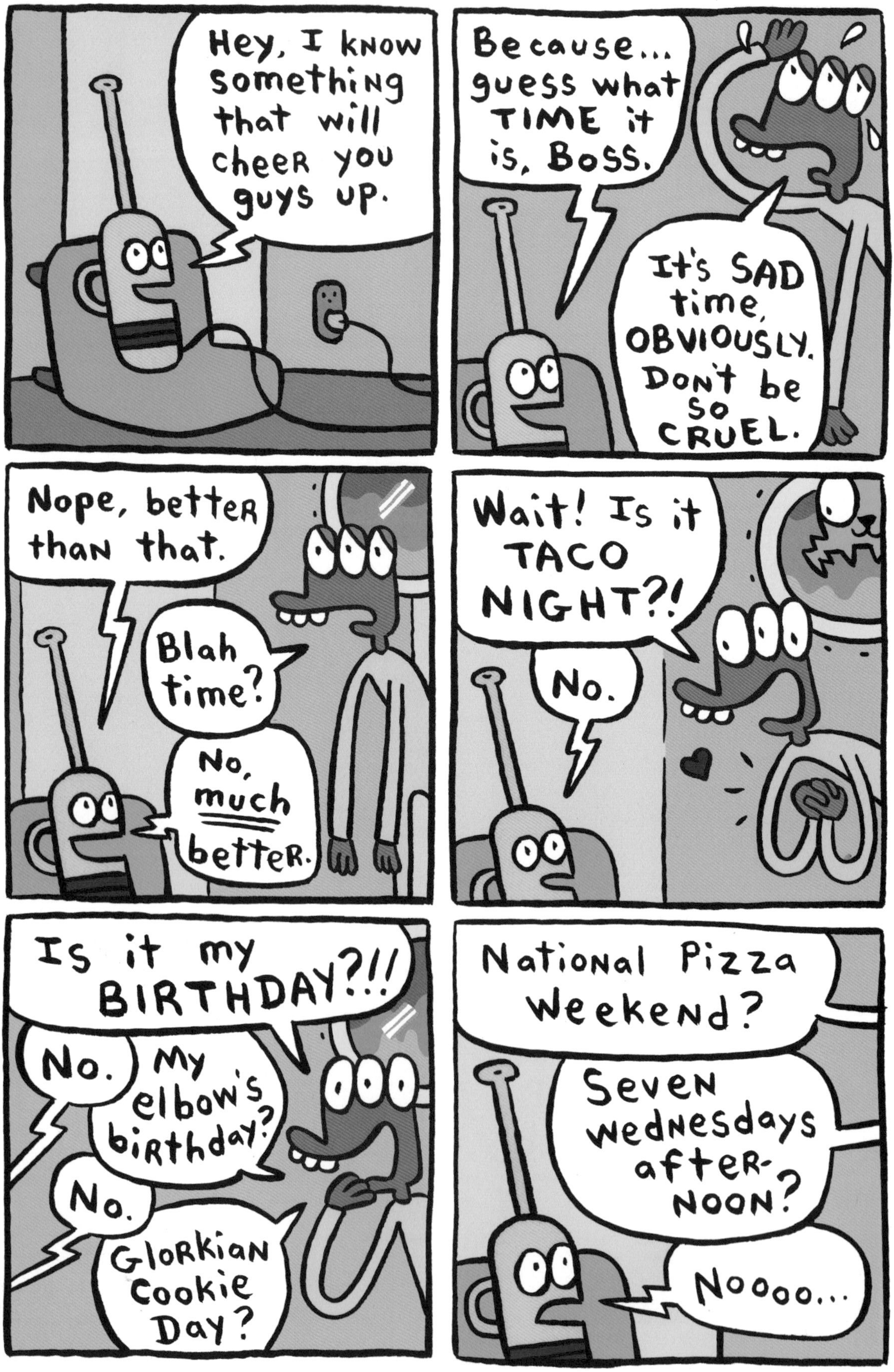
Hey, I know something that will cheer you guys up.
Because... guess what TIME it is, Boss.
It's SAD time, OBVIOUSLY. Don't be so CRUEL.
Nope, better than that.
Blah time?
No, much better.
Wait! Is it TACO NIGHT?!
No.
Is it my BIRTHDAY?!!
No.
My elbow's birthday?
No.
Glorkian Cookie Day?
National Pizza Weekend?
Seven wednesdays after-noon?
Noooo...

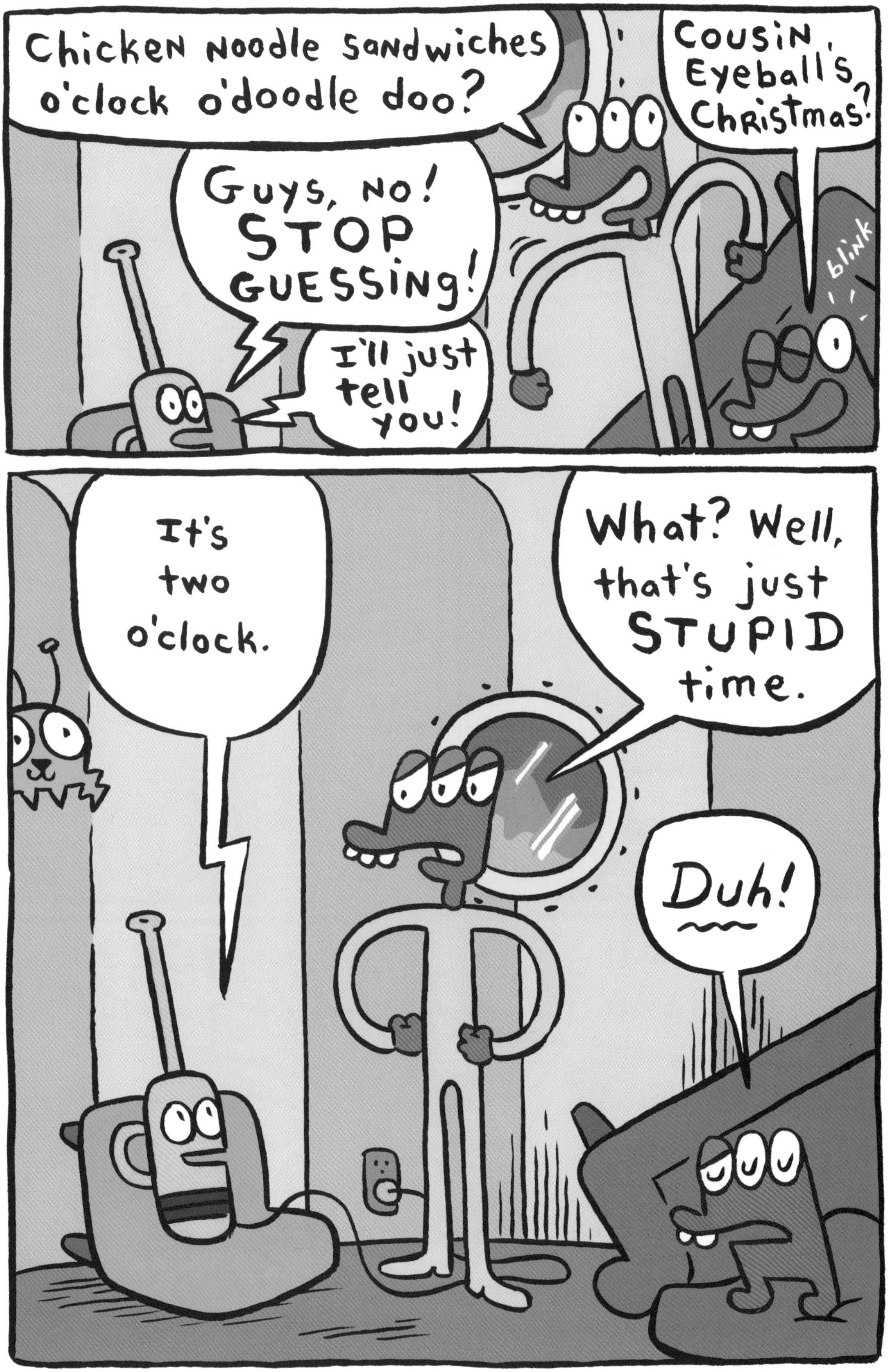
Chicken noodle sandwiches o'clock o'doodle doo?
Cousin Eyeball's Christmas?
blink
Guys, no! STOP GUESSING!
I'll just tell you!
It's two o'clock.
What? Well, that's just STUPID time.
Duh!

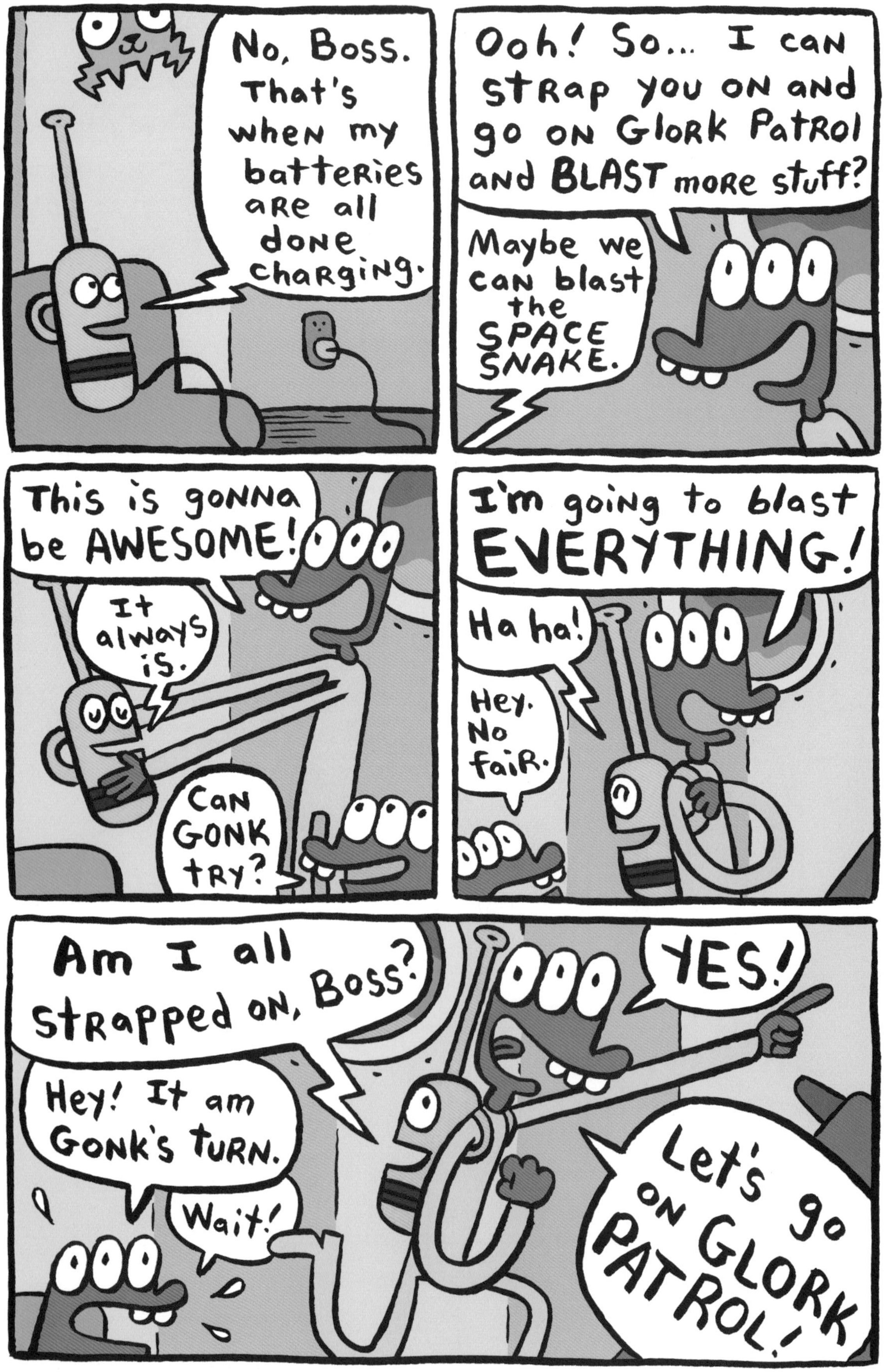

No, Boss. That's when my batteries are all done charging.
Ooh! So... I can strap you on and go on Glork Patrol and BLAST more stuff?
Maybe we can blast the SPACE SNAKE.
This is gonna be AWESOME!
It always is.
Can GONK try?
I'm going to blast EVERYTHING!
Ha ha!
Hey. No fair.
Am I all strapped on, Boss?
YES!
Hey! It am Gonk's turn.
Wait!
Let's go on GLORK PATROL!

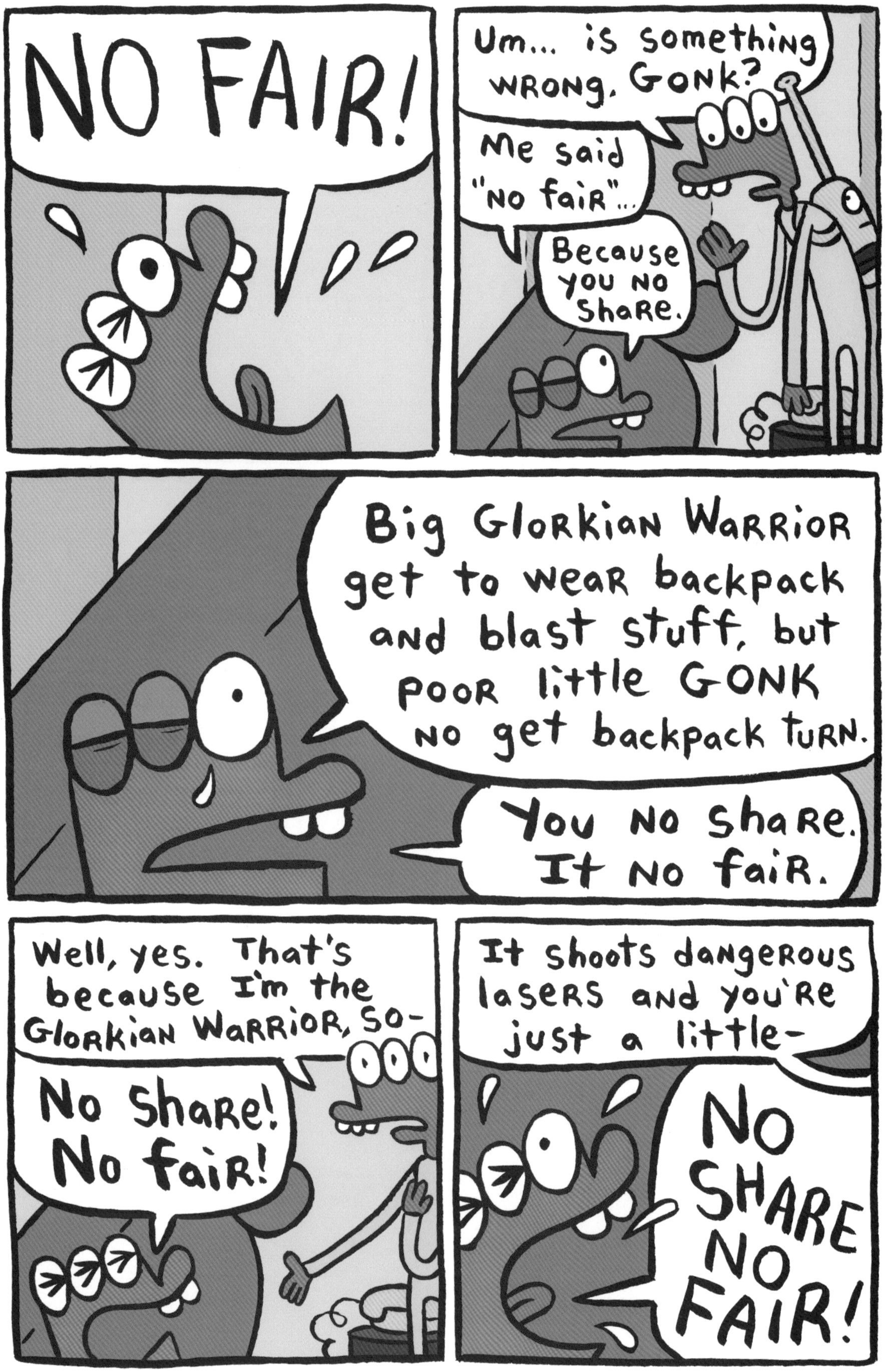
NO FAIR!
Um... is something wrong, GONK?
Me said "no fair"...
Because you no share.
Big Glorkian Warrior get to wear backpack and blast stuff, but poor little GONK no get backpack turn.
You no share. It no fair.
Well, yes. That's because I'm the Glorkian Warrior, so-
No share! No fair!
It shoots dangerous lasers and you're just a little-
NO SHARE NO FAIR!

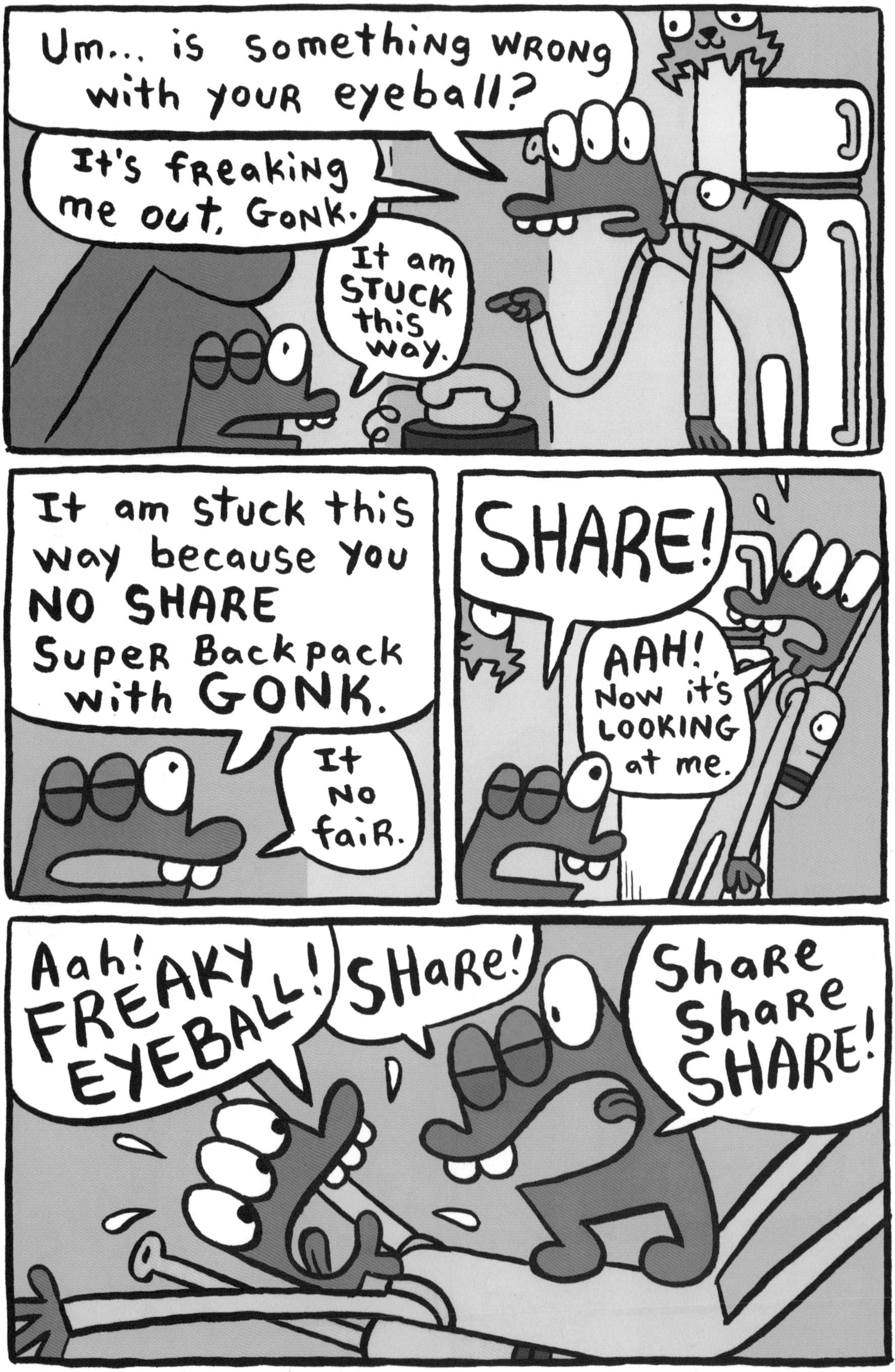

Um... is something WRONG with your eyeball?
It's freaking me out, GONK.
It am STUCK this way.
It am stuck this way because you NO SHARE Super Backpack with GONK.
It NO fair.
SHARE!
AAH! Now it's LOOKING at me.
Aah! FREAKY EYEBALL!
SHare!
Share Share SHARE!

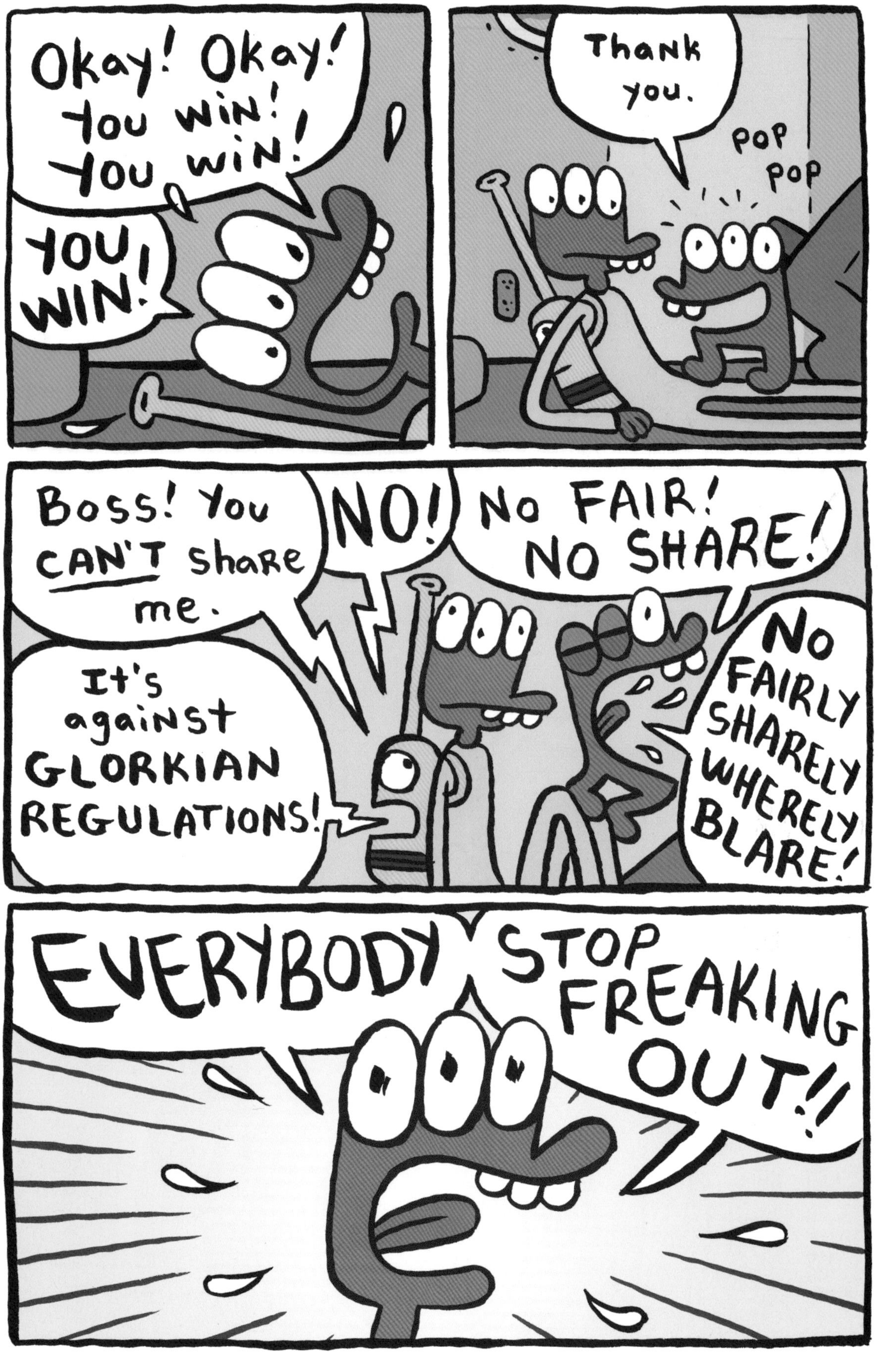

Okay! Okay! You win! You win!
YOU WIN!
Thank you.
POP POP
Boss! You CAN'T share me.
It's against GLORKIAN REGULATIONS!
NO!
NO FAIR! NO SHARE!
NO FAIRLY SHARELY WHERELY BLARE!
EVERYBODY STOP FREAKING OUT!!

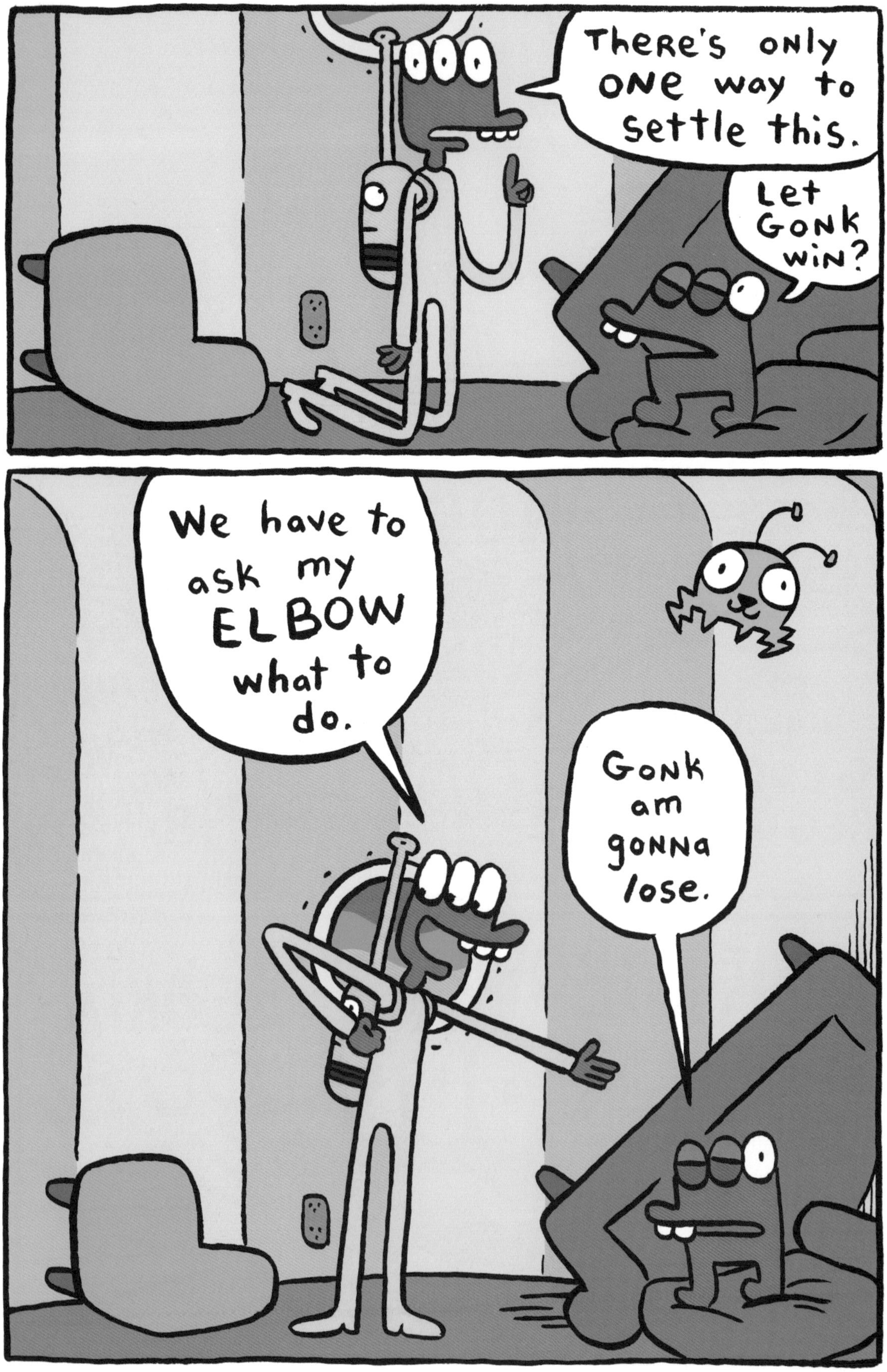
There's only ONE way to settle this.
Let GONK win?
We have to ask my ELBOW what to do.
GONK am gonna lose.

CHAPTER FIVE

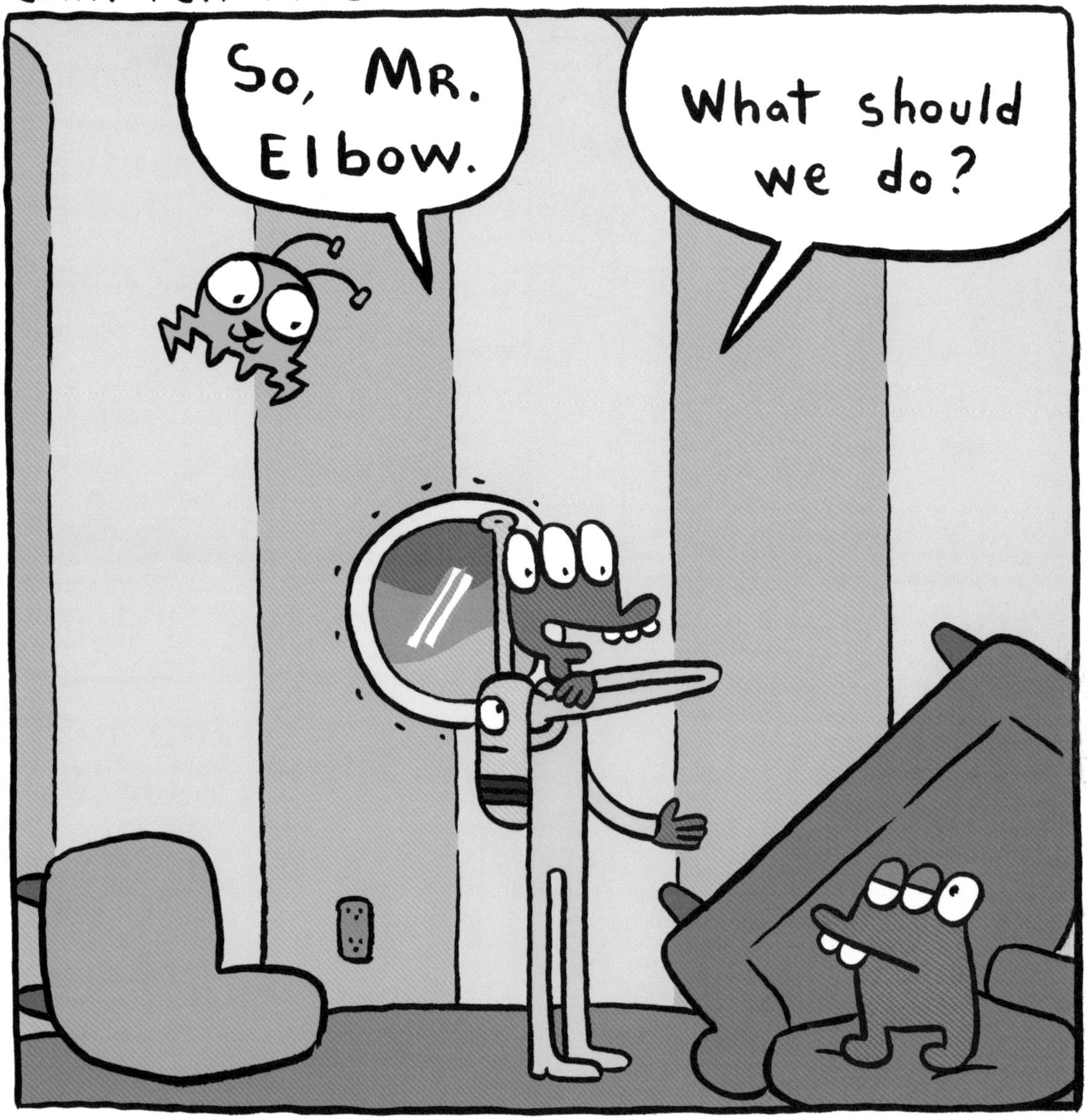
So, Mr. Elbow.
What should we do?

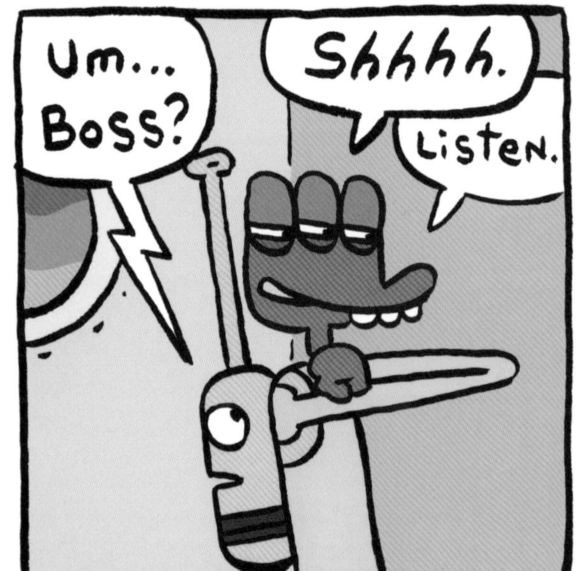
Um... Boss?
Shhhh.
Listen.

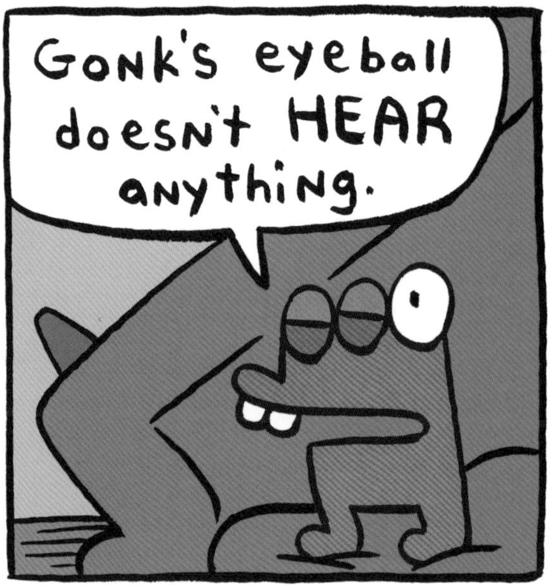
Gonk's eyeball doesn't HEAR anything.

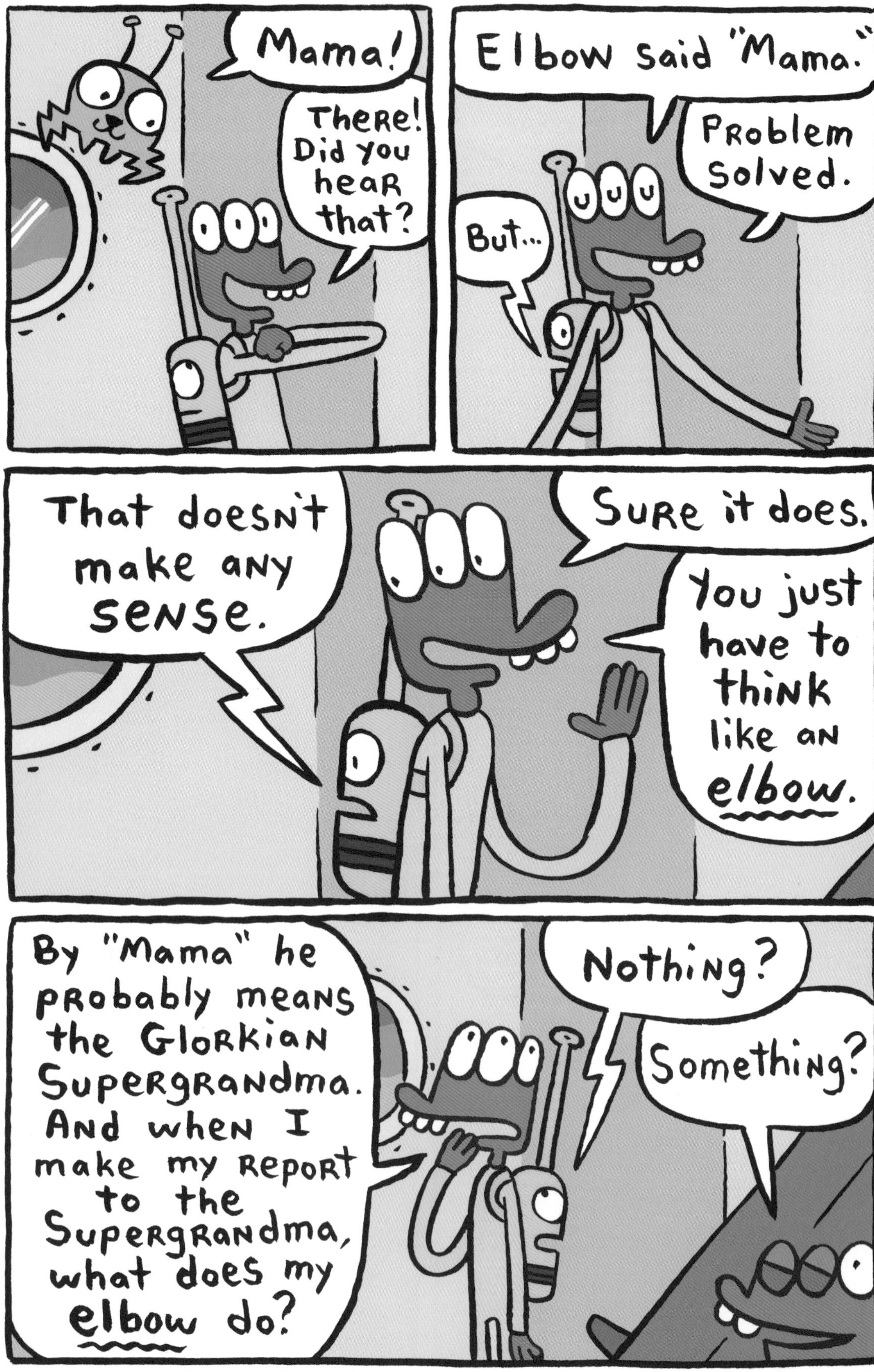

Mama!
There! Did you hear that?
Elbow said "Mama."
Problem solved.
But...
That doesn't make any sense.
Sure it does.
You just have to think like an elbow.
By "Mama" he probably means the Glorkian Supergrandma. And when I make my report to the Supergrandma, what does my elbow do?
Nothing?
Something?

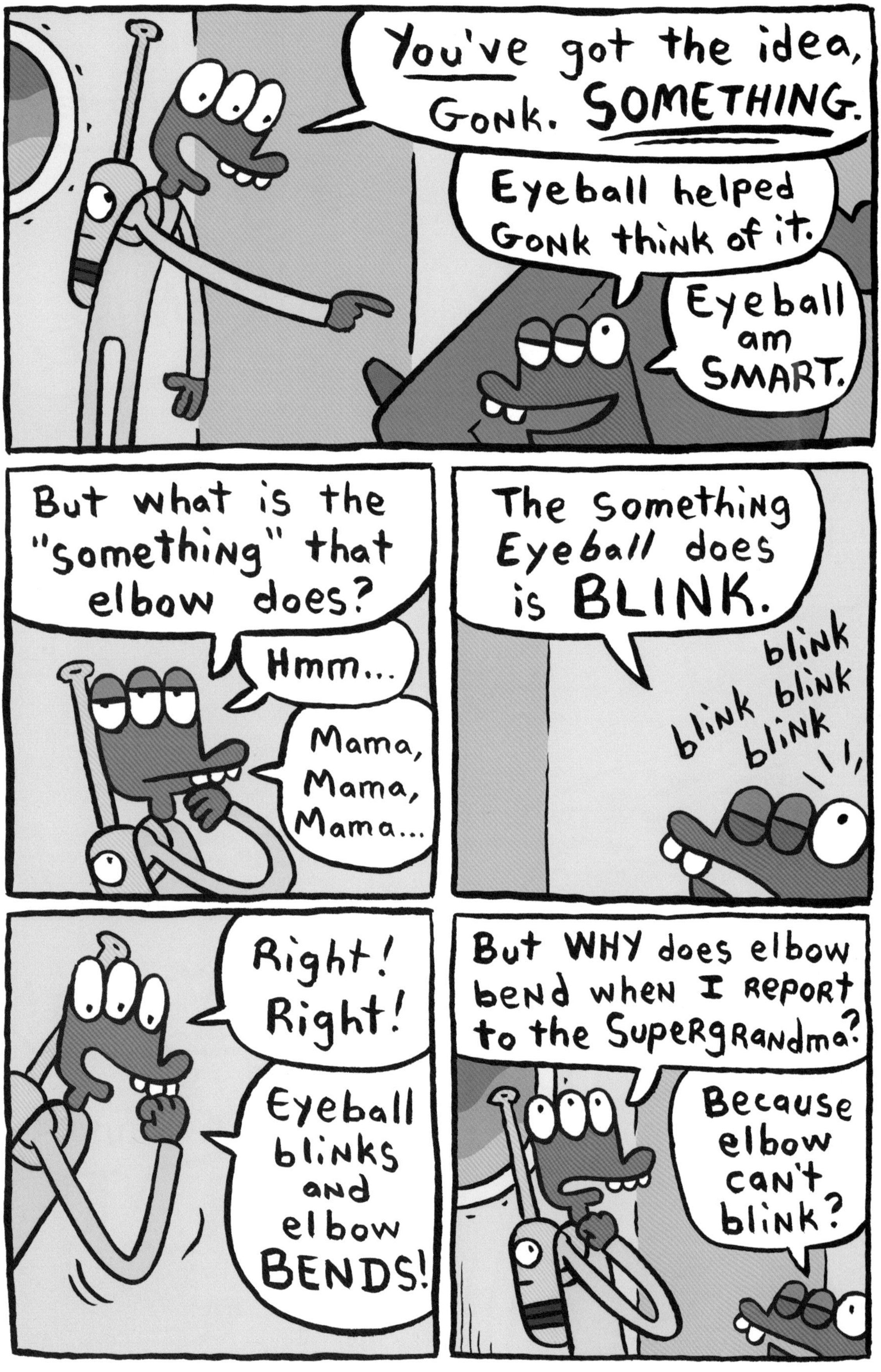
You've got the idea, Gonk. SOMETHING.
Eyeball helped Gonk think of it.
Eyeball am SMART.
But what is the "something" that elbow does?
Hmm...
Mama, Mama, Mama...
The something Eyeball does is BLINK.
blink blink blink blink
Right! Right!
Eyeball blinks and elbow BENDS!
But WHY does elbow bend when I report to the Supergrandma?
Because elbow can't blink?

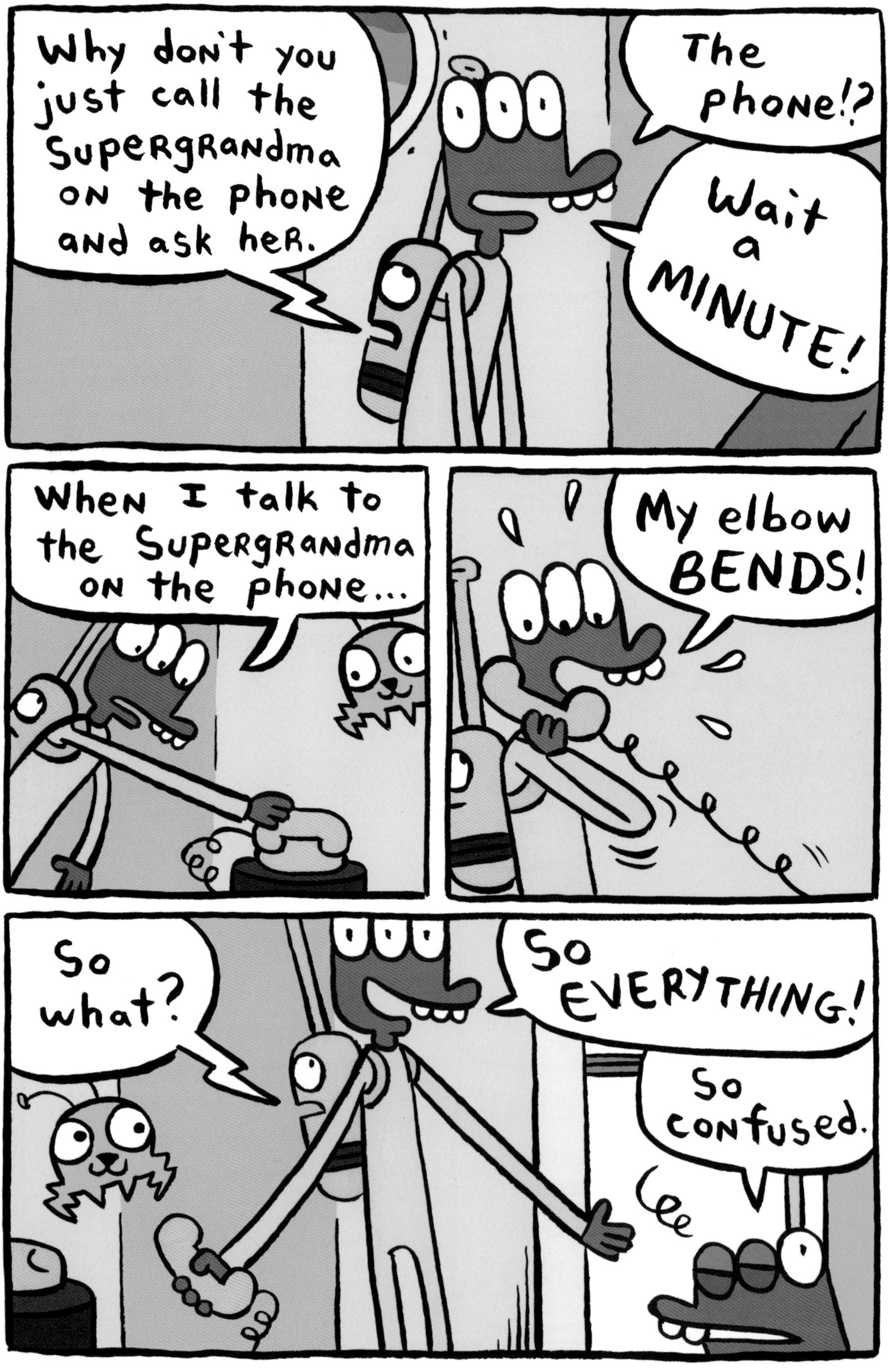
Why don't you just call the Supergrandma on the phone and ask her.
The phone!?
Wait a MINUTE!
When I talk to the Supergrandma on the phone...
My elbow BENDS!
So what?
So EVERYTHING!
So confused.

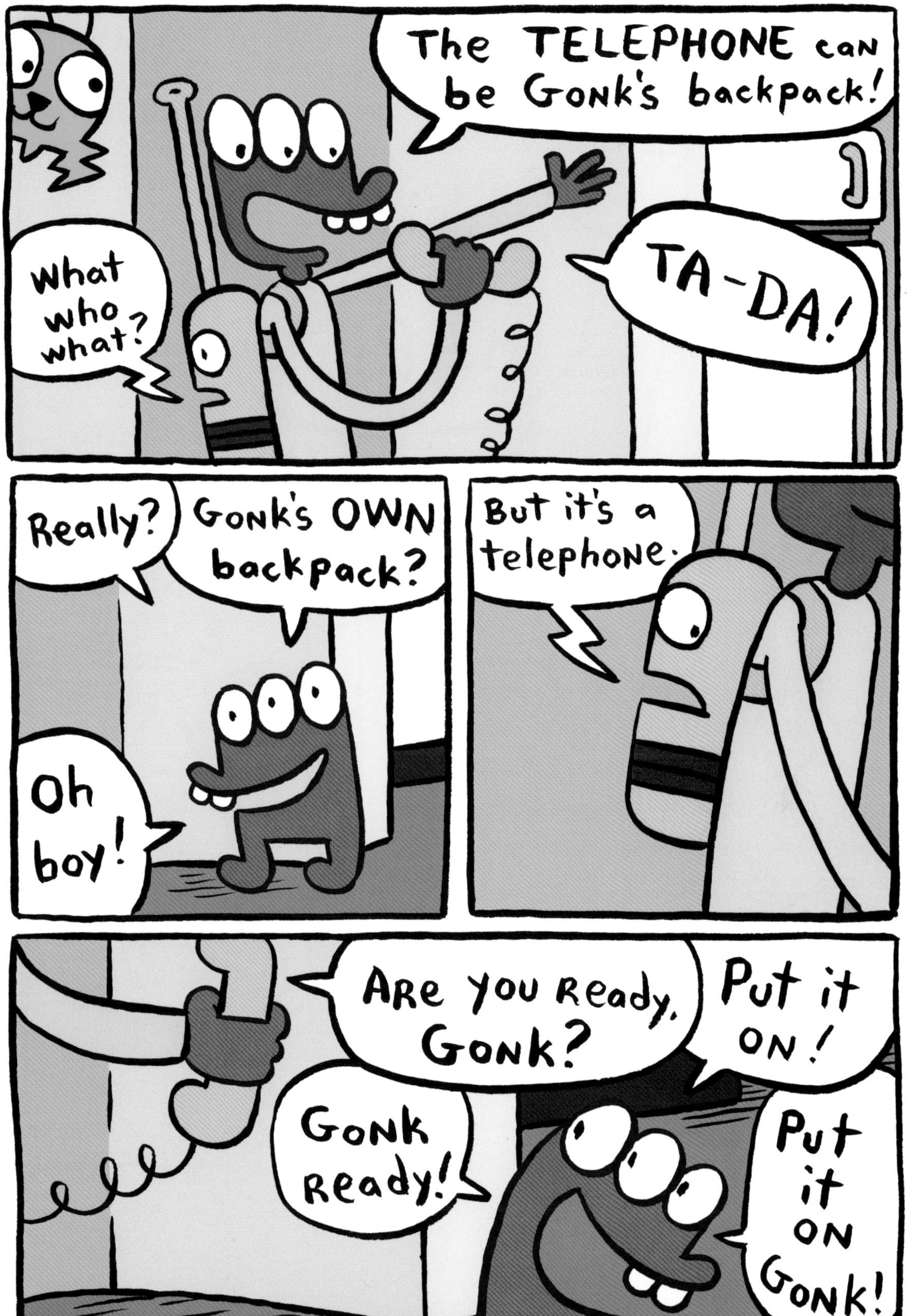
The TELEPHONE can be Gonk's backpack!
What who what?
TA-DA!
Really?
Gonk's OWN backpack?
Oh boy!
But it's a telephone.
Are you ready, Gonk?
Gonk ready!
Put it ON!
Put it ON Gonk!

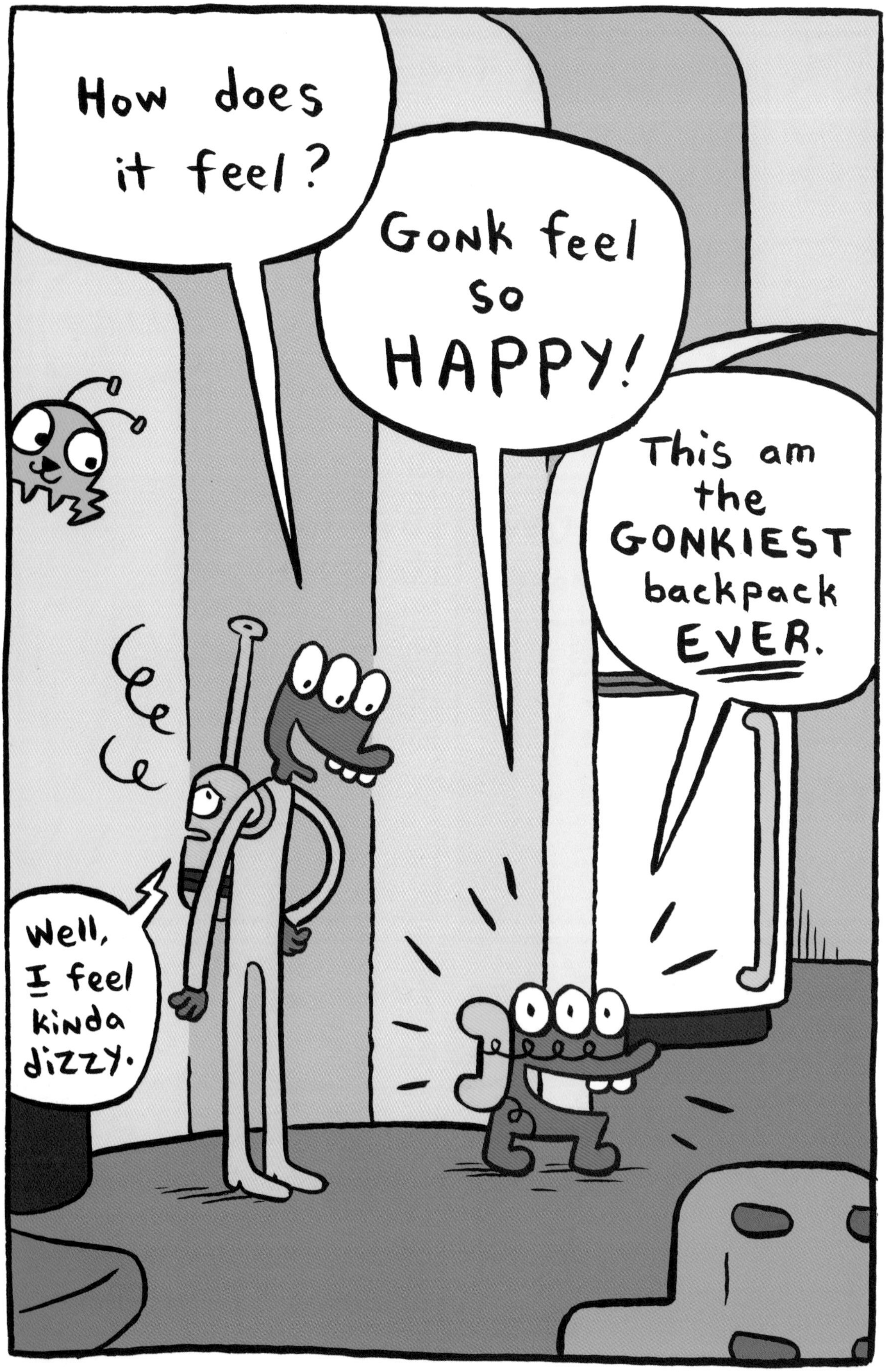
How does it feel?
Gonk feel so HAPPY!
This am the GONKIEST backpack EVER.
Well, I feel kinda dizzy.

CHAPTER SIX

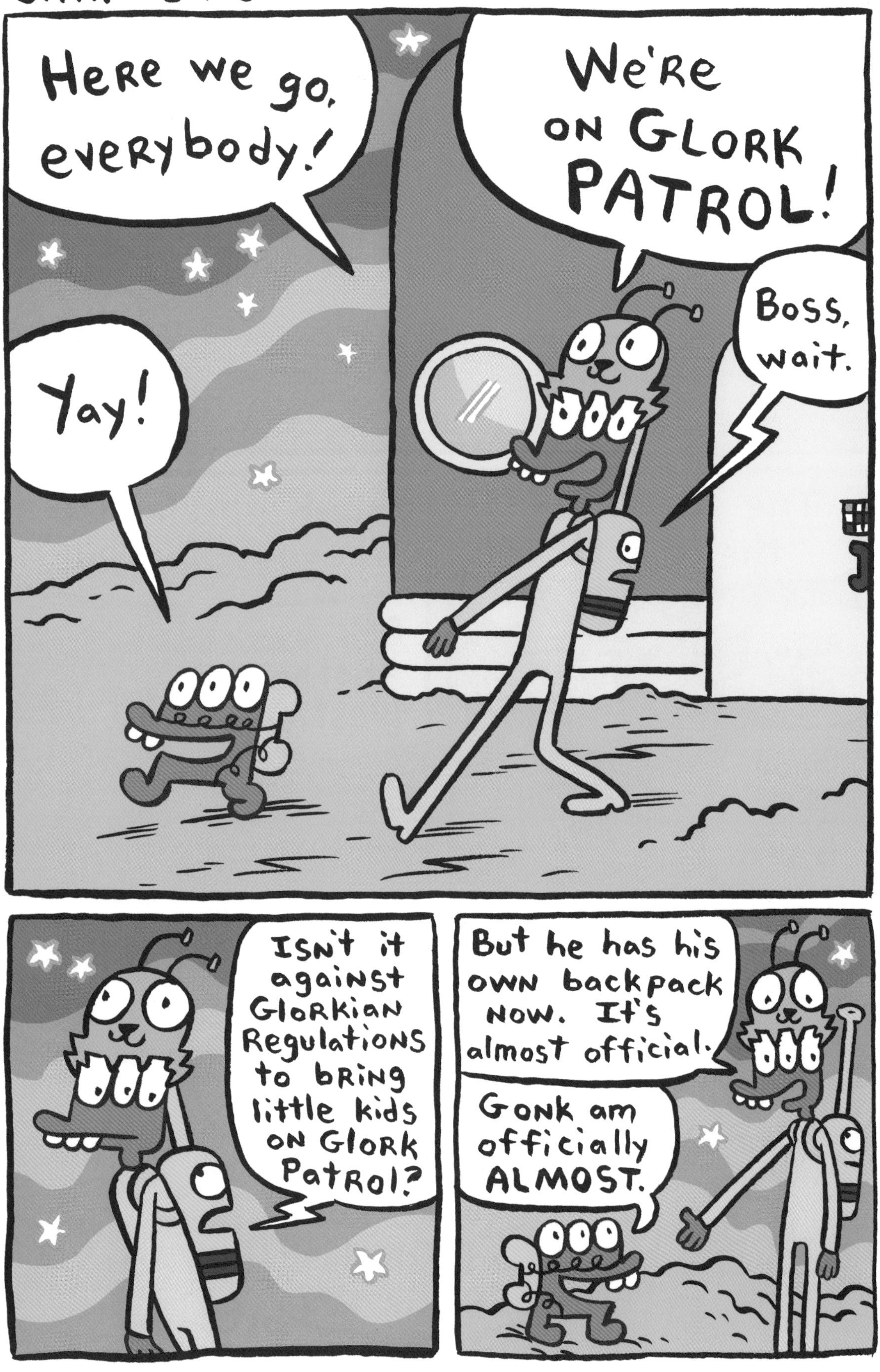

Here we go, everybody!
We're on GLORK PATROL!
Yay!
Boss, wait.
Isn't it against Glorkian Regulations to bring little kids on Glork Patrol?
But he has his own backpack now. It's almost official.
Gonk am officially ALMOST.

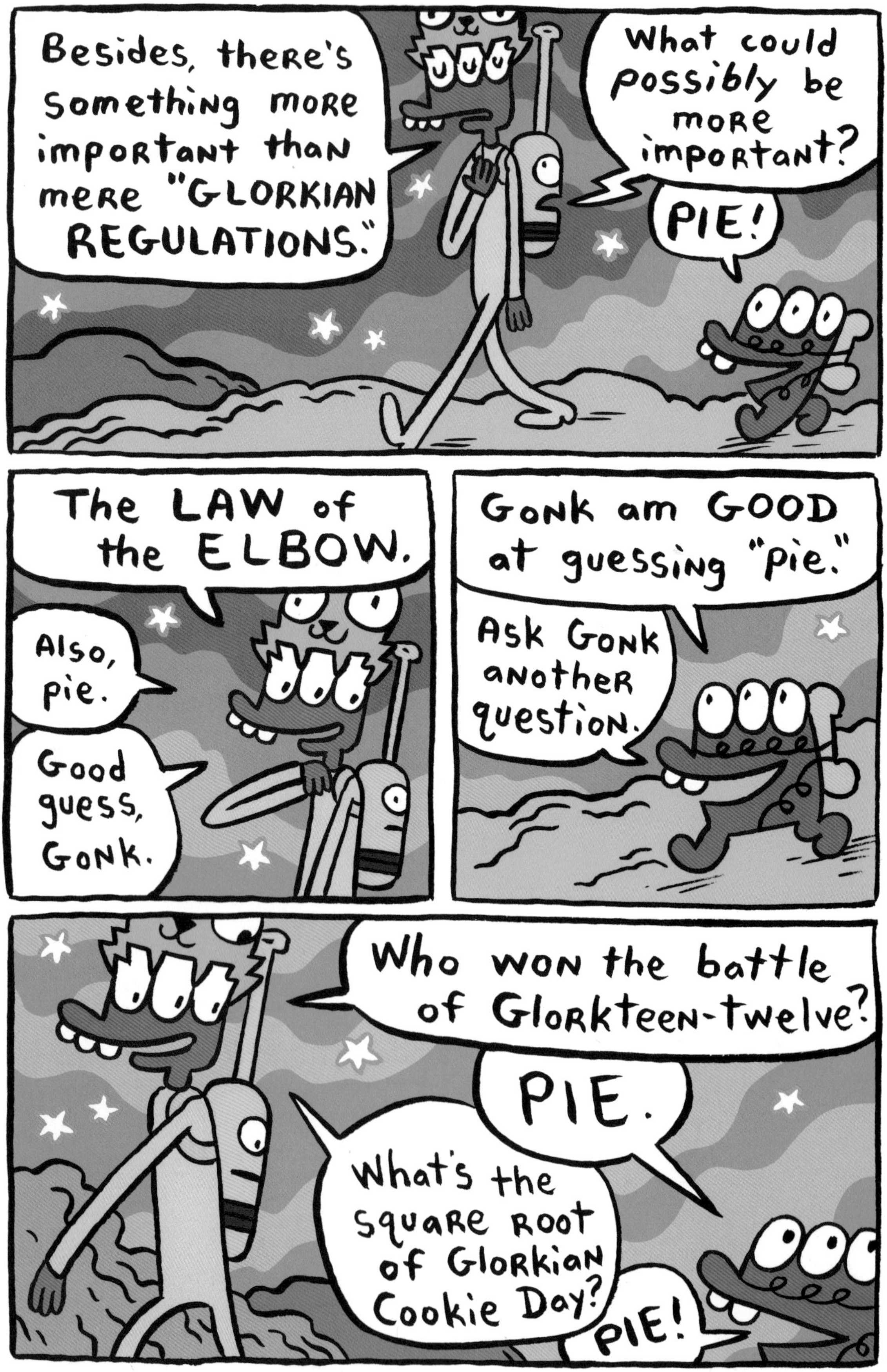
Besides, there's something more important than mere "GLORKIAN REGULATIONS."
What could possibly be more important?
PIE!
The LAW of the ELBOW.
Also, pie.
Good guess, Gonk.
Gonk am GOOD at guessing "pie."
Ask Gonk another question.
Who won the battle of Glorkteen-twelve?
PIE.
What's the square root of Glorkian Cookie Day?
PIE!

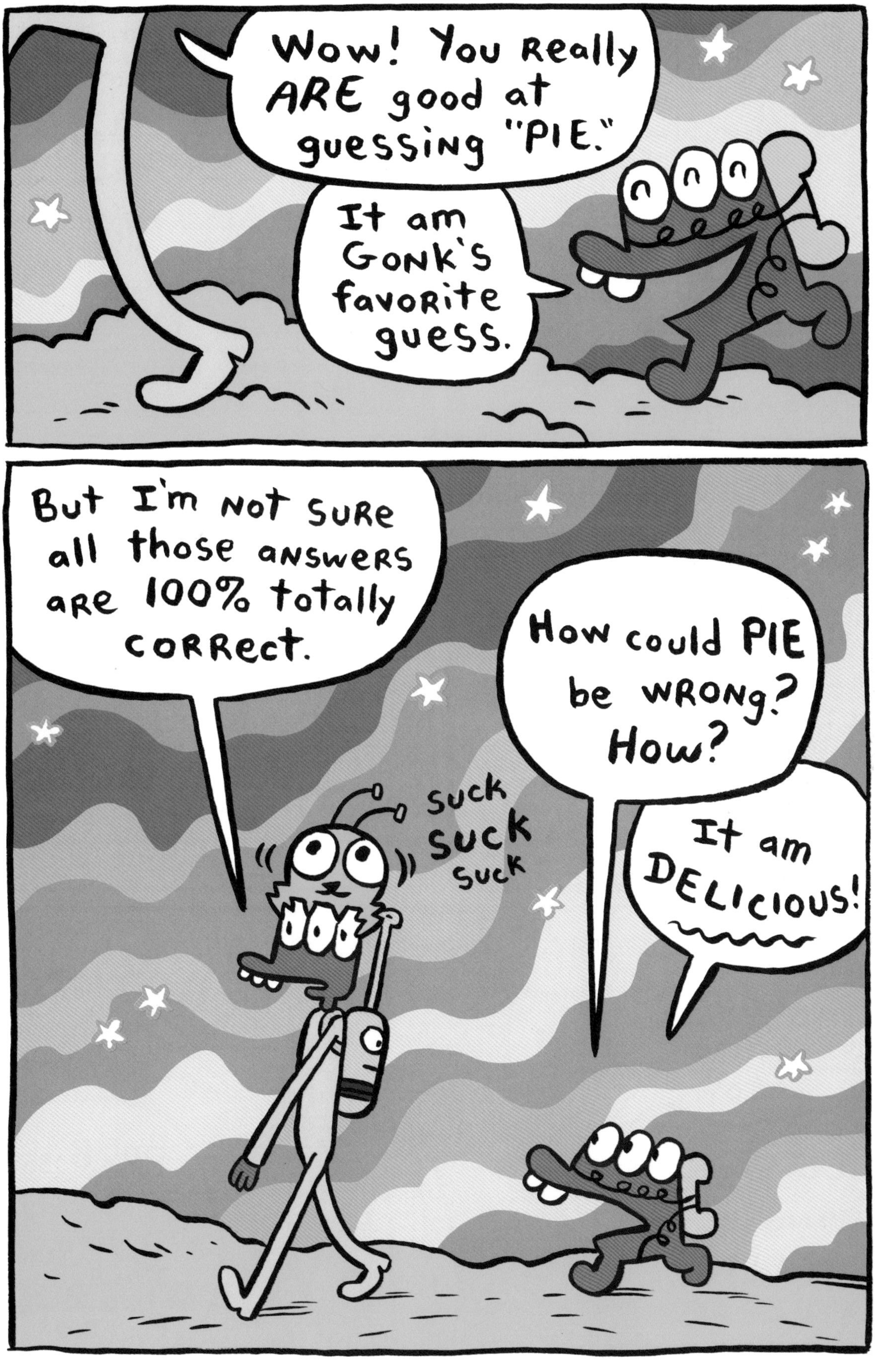
Wow! You really ARE good at guessing "PIE."
It am Gonk's favorite guess.
But I'm not sure all those answers are 100% totally correct.
How could PIE be wrong? How?
It am DELICIOUS!
suck suck suck

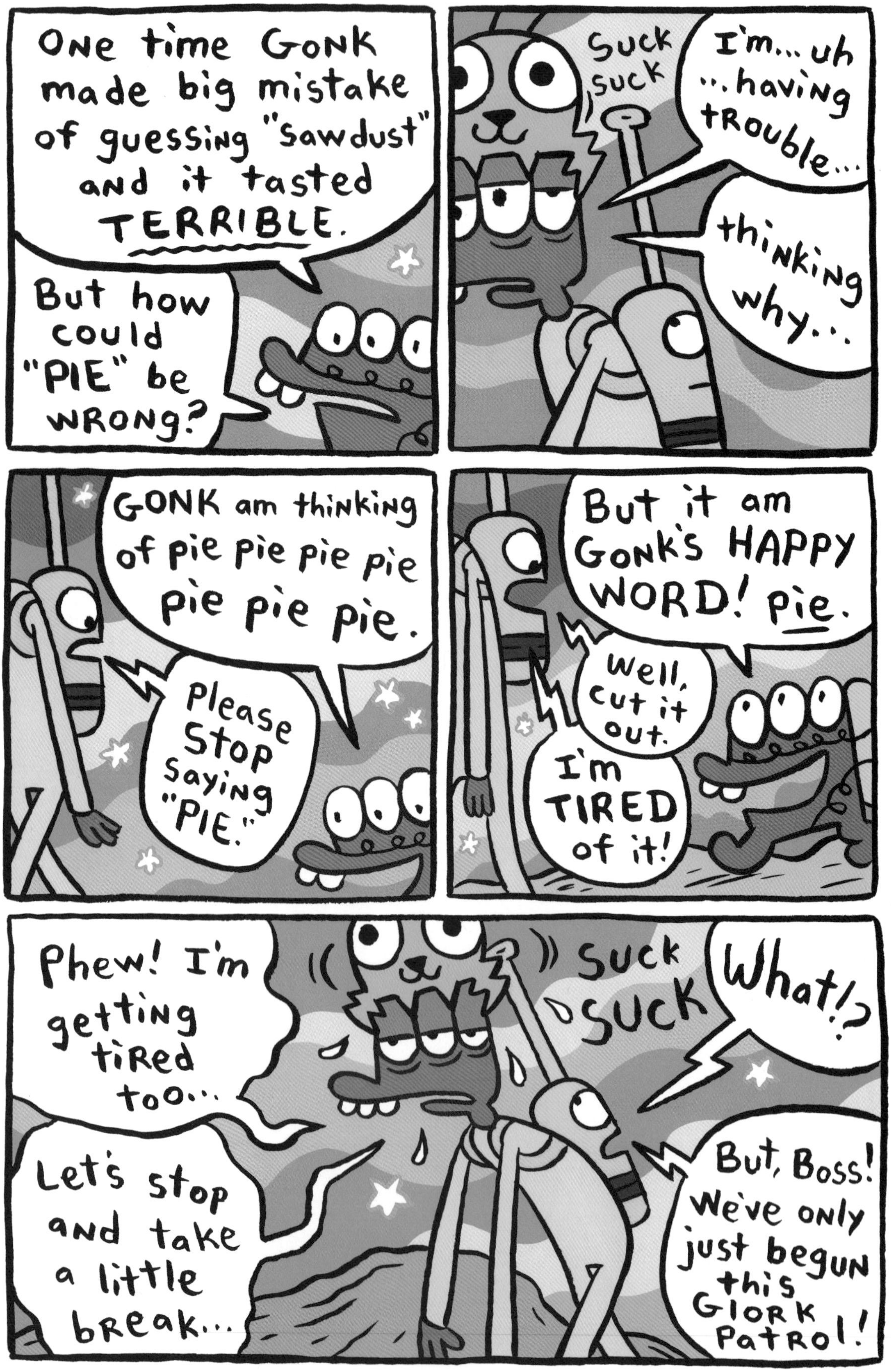
One time Gonk made big mistake of guessing "sawdust" and it tasted TERRIBLE.
But how could "PIE" be wrong?
Suck suck
I'm... uh ...having trouble...
thinking why...
GONK am thinking of pie pie pie pie pie pie pie.
Please stop saying "PIE."
But it am Gonk's HAPPY WORD! pie.
Well, cut it out.
I'm TIRED of it!
Phew! I'm getting tired too...
Let's stop and take a little break...
Suck SUCK
What!?
But, Boss! We've only just begun this Glork Patrol!

CHAPTER SEVEN

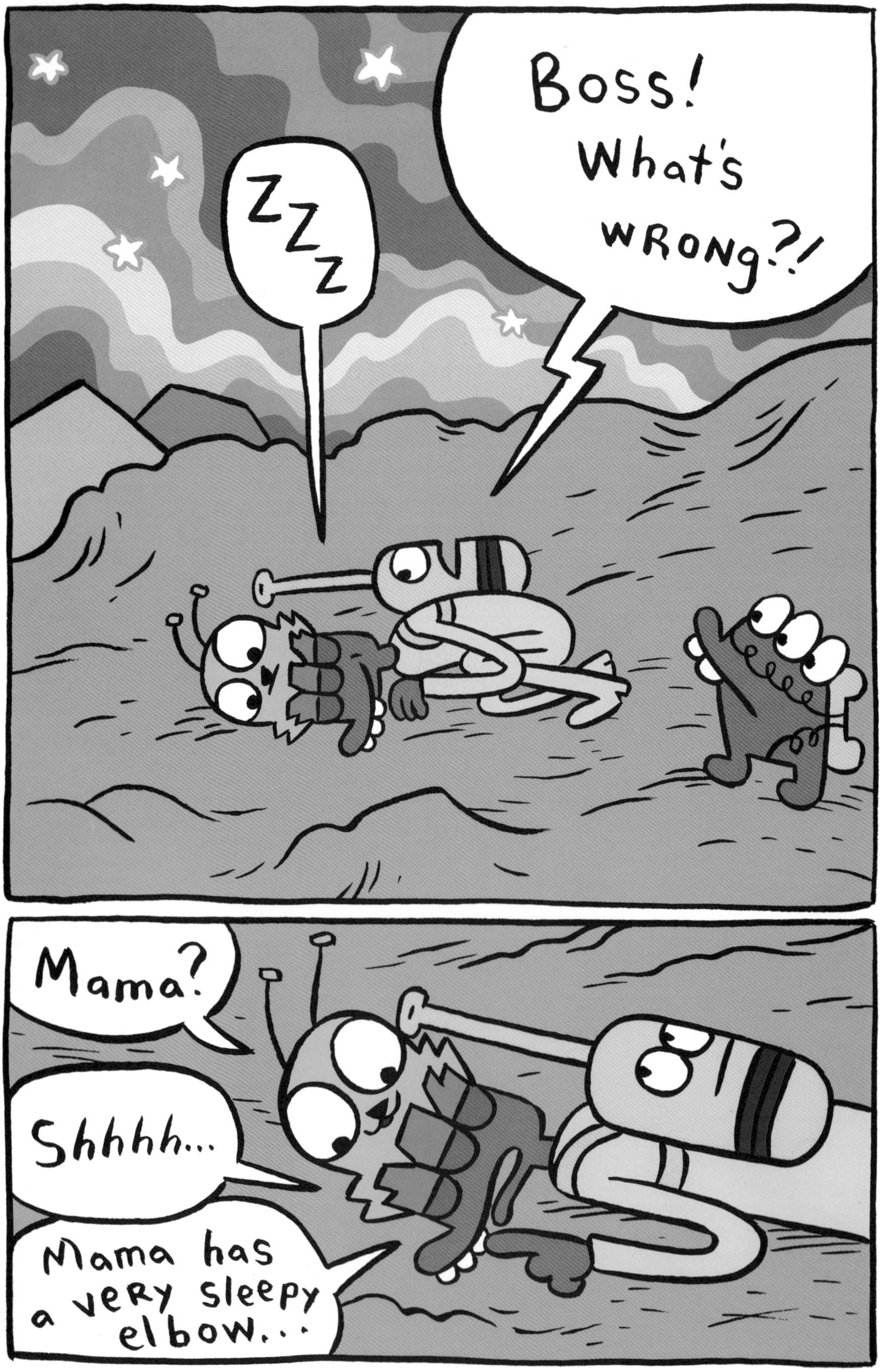
Boss! What's WRONG?!
ZZZ
Mama?
Shhhh...
Mama has a very sleepy elbow...

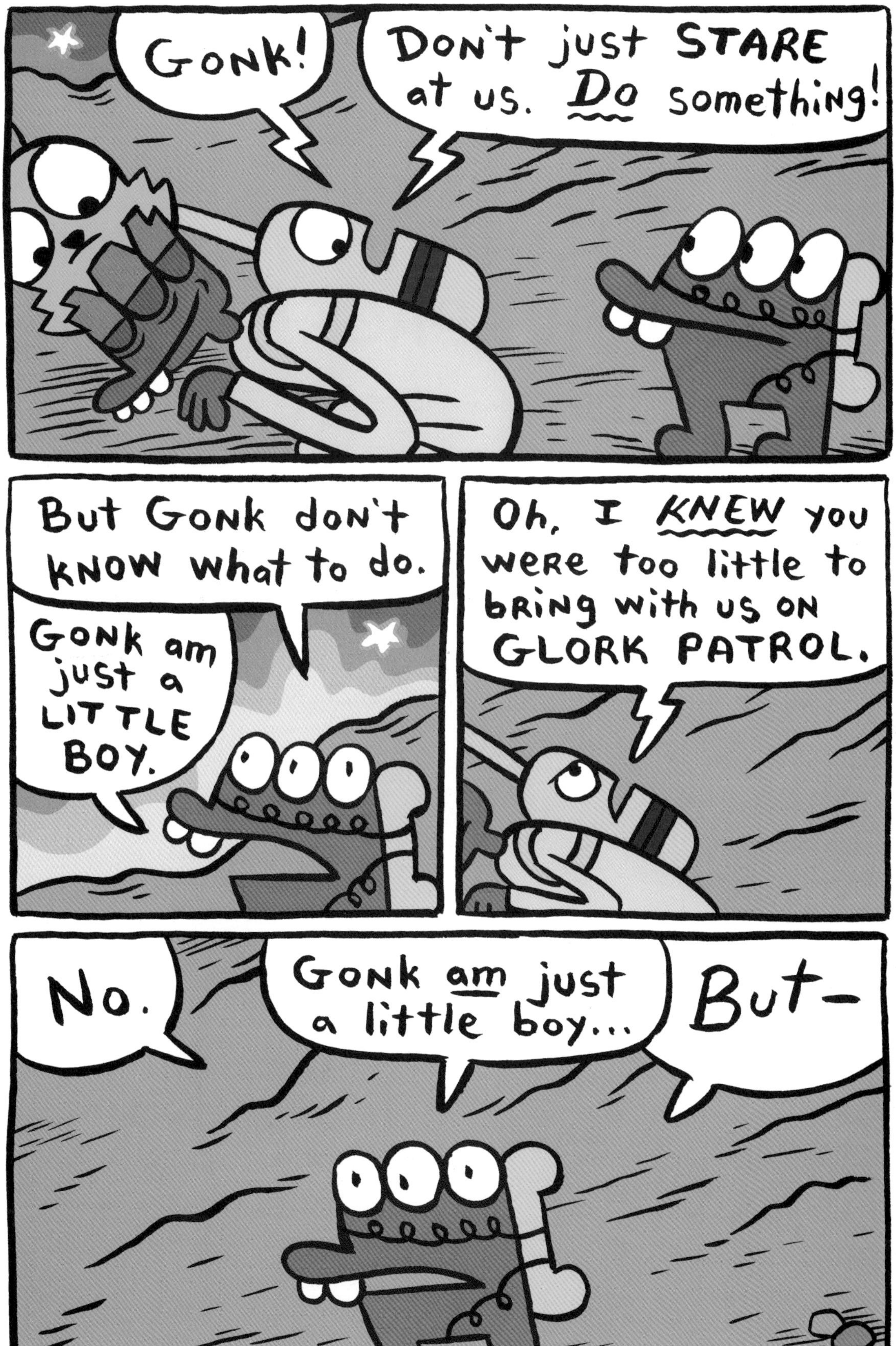
GONK!
Don't just STARE at us. DO something!
But Gonk don't KNOW what to do.
Gonk am just a LITTLE BOY.
Oh, I KNEW you were too little to bring with us on GLORK PATROL.
No.
Gonk am just a little boy...
But-

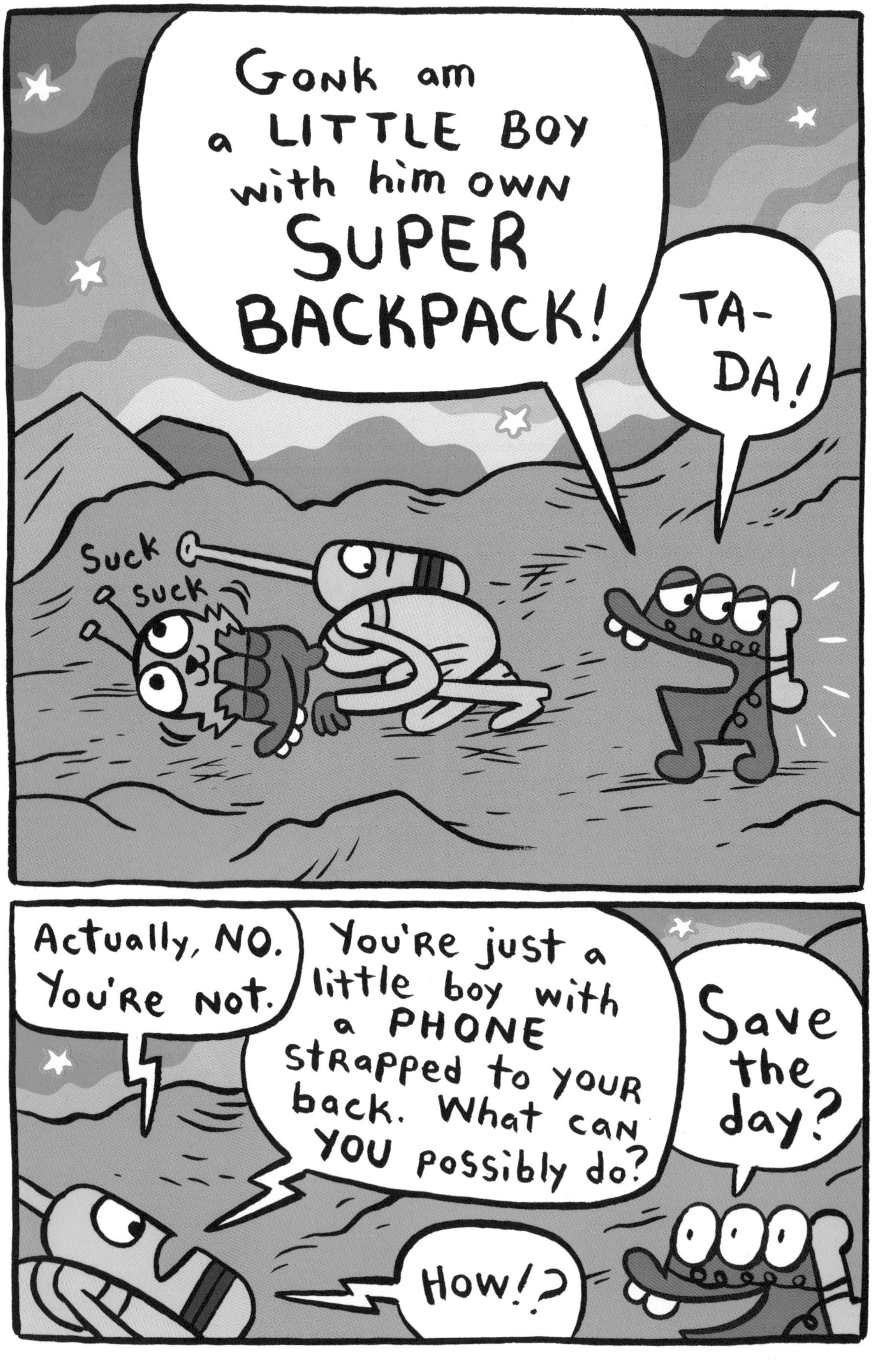
Gonk am a LITTLE BOY with him own SUPER BACKPACK!
TA-DA!
Suck suck
Actually, NO. You're not.
You're just a little boy with a PHONE strapped to your back. What can YOU possibly do?
Save the day?
How!?

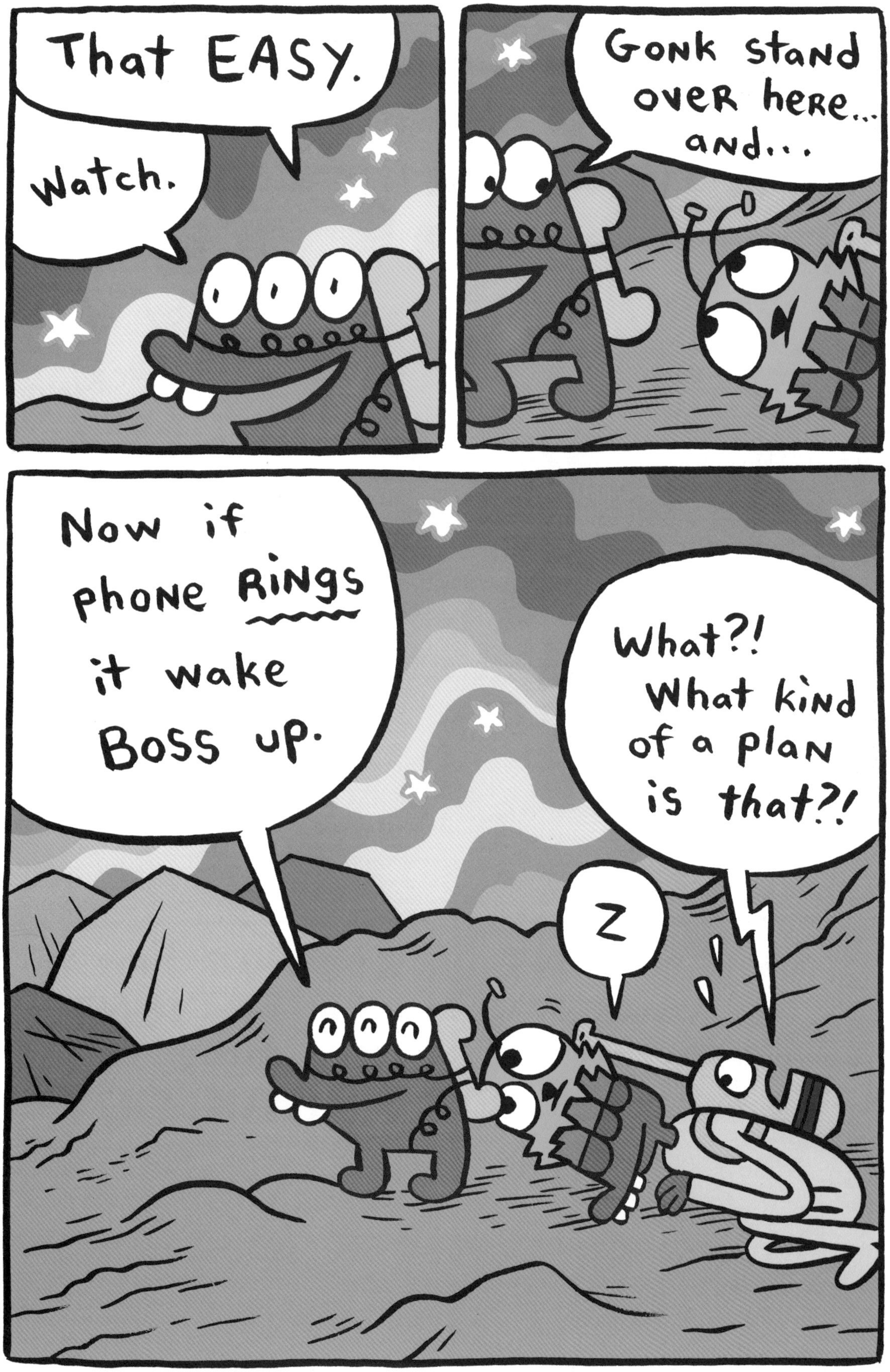
That EASY.
Watch.
Gonk stand over here... and...
Now if phone RINGS it wake Boss up.
What?! What kind of a plan is that?!
Z

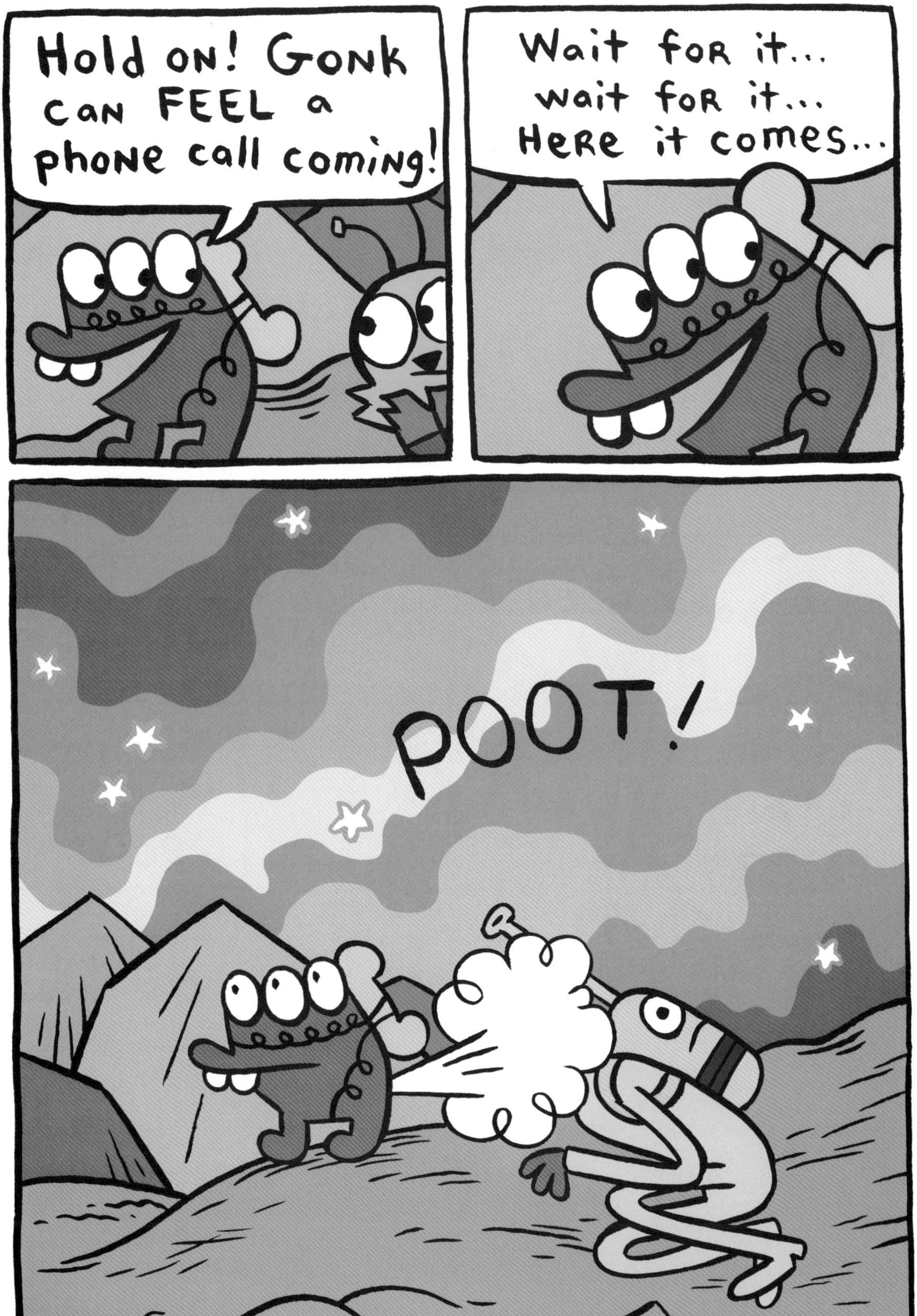
Hold on! Gonk can FEEL a phone call coming!
Wait for it... wait for it... Here it comes...
POOT!

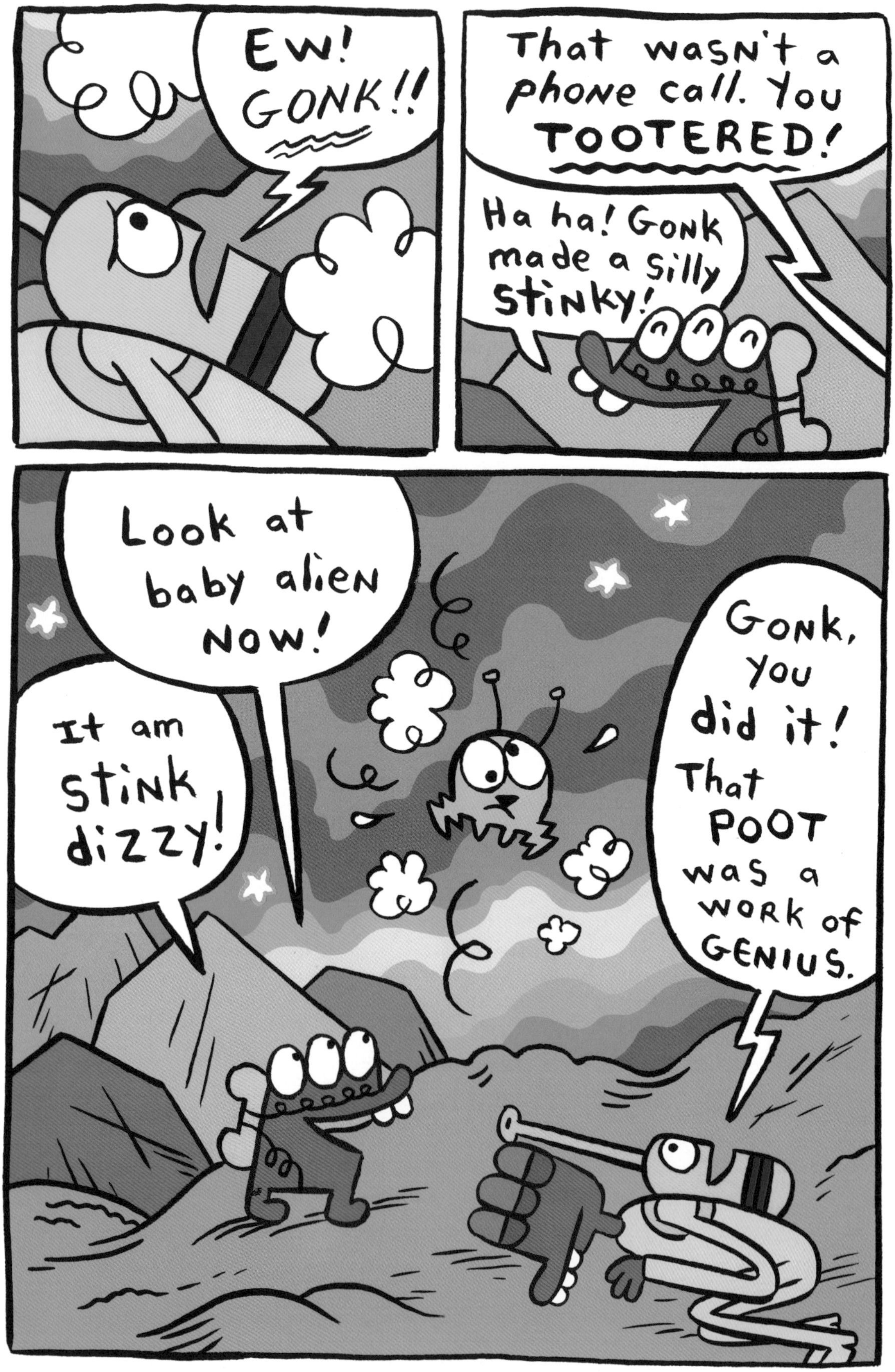
Ew! GONK!!
That wasn't a phone call. You TOOTERED!
Ha ha! Gonk made a silly stinky!
Look at baby alien now!
It am stink dizzy!
Gonk, you did it! That POOT was a work of GENIUS.

CHAPTER NINE

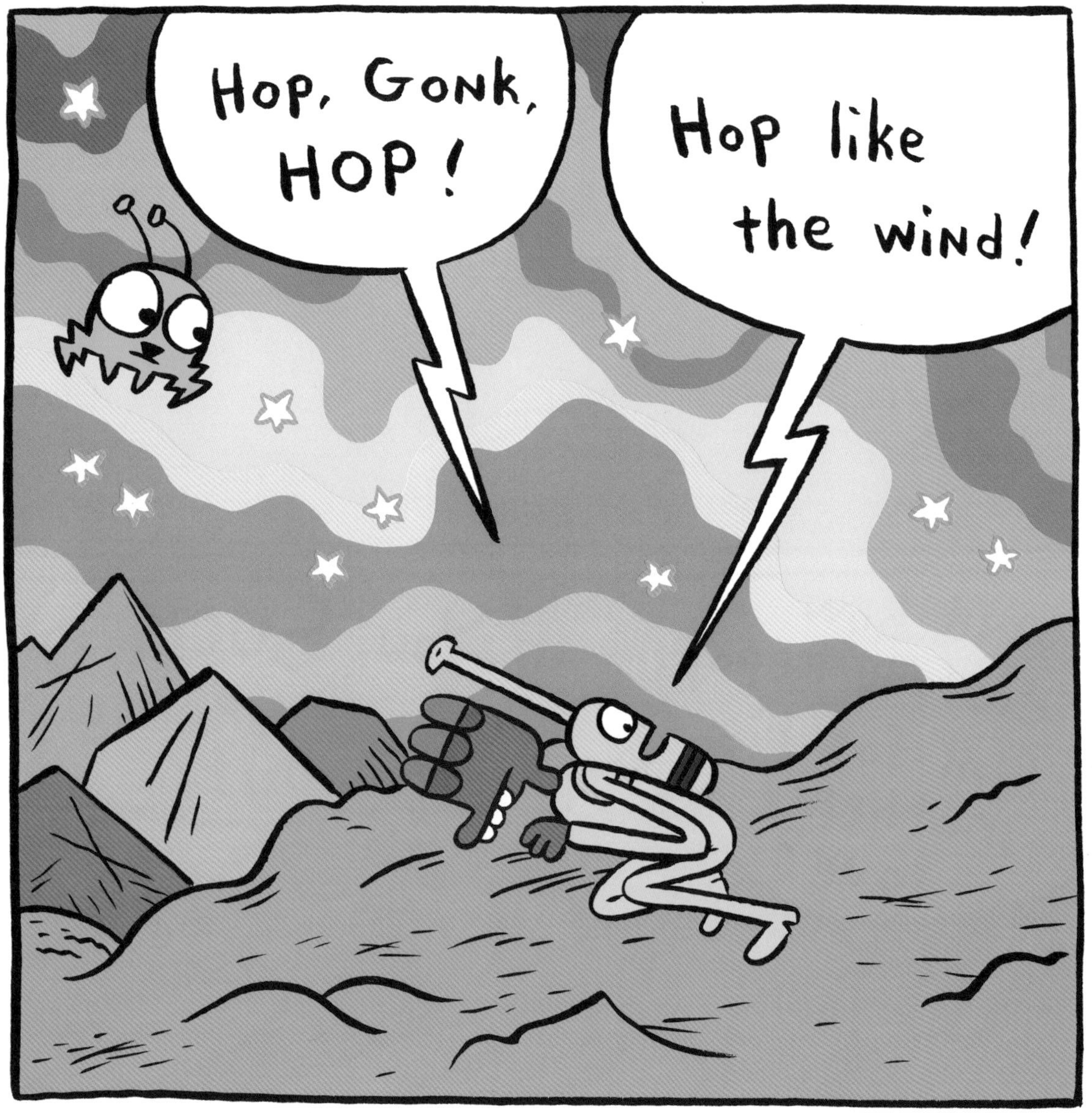
Hop, Gonk, HOP!
Hop like the wind!

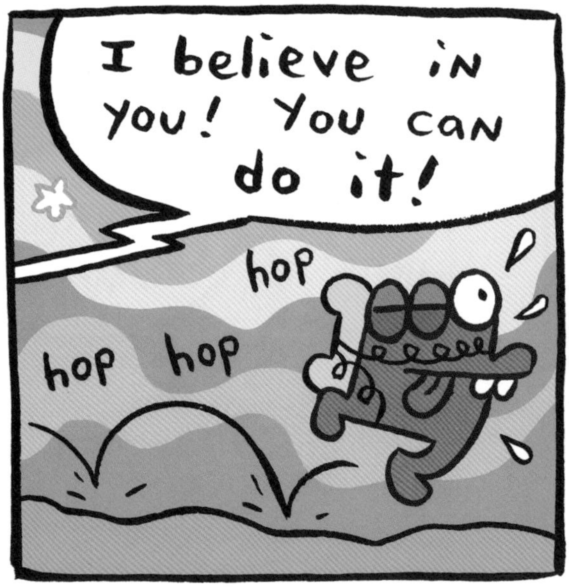
I believe in you! You can do it!
hop
hop hop

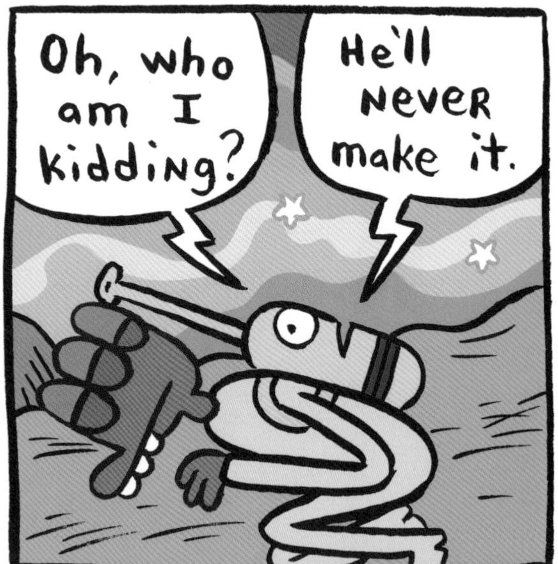
Oh, who am I kidding?
He'll never make it.

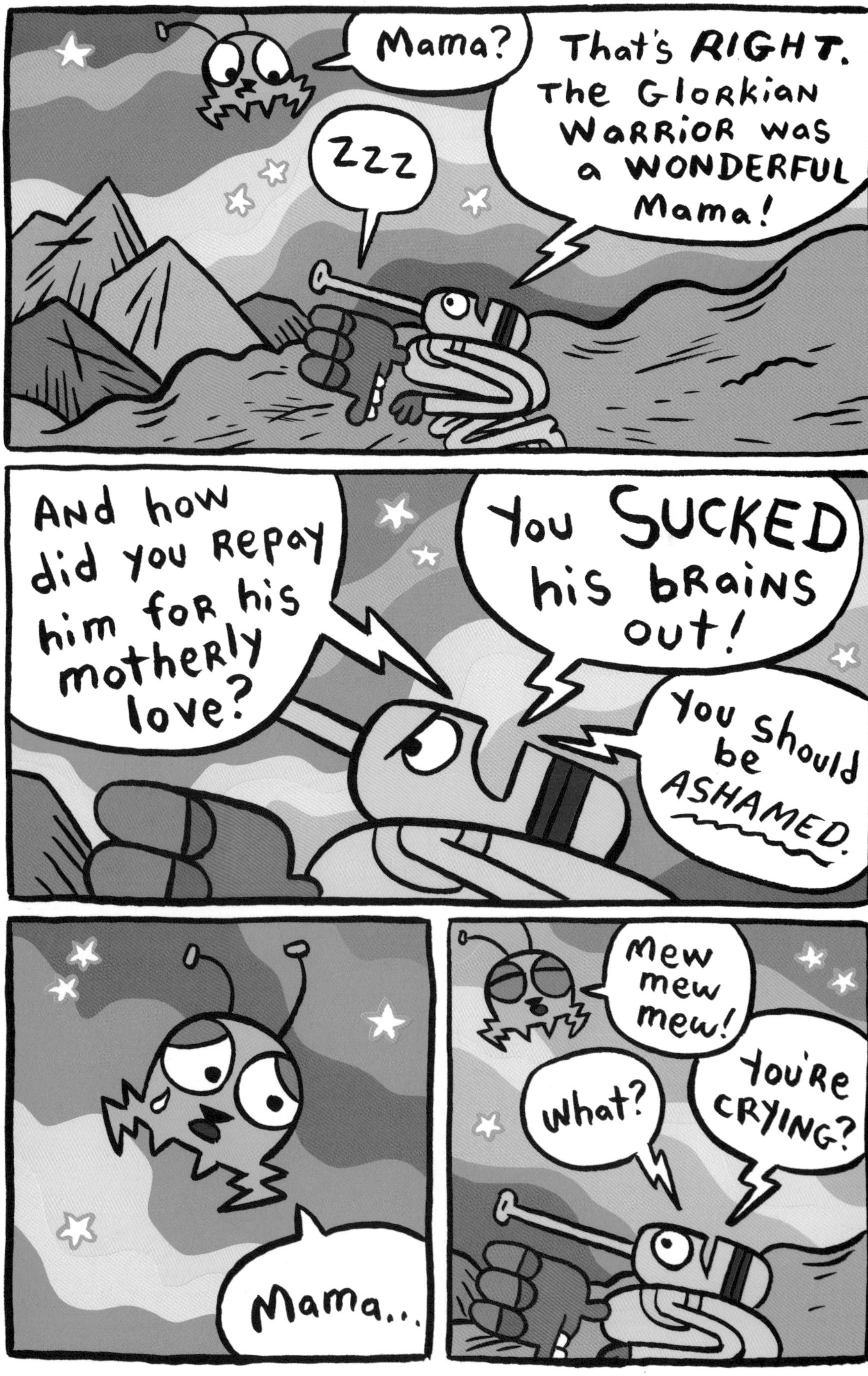
Mama?
ZZZ
That's RIGHT. The Glorkian Warrior was a WONDERFUL Mama!
And how did you repay him for his motherly love?
You SUCKED his brains out!
You should be ASHAMED.
Mama...
Mew mew mew!
What?
You're CRYING?

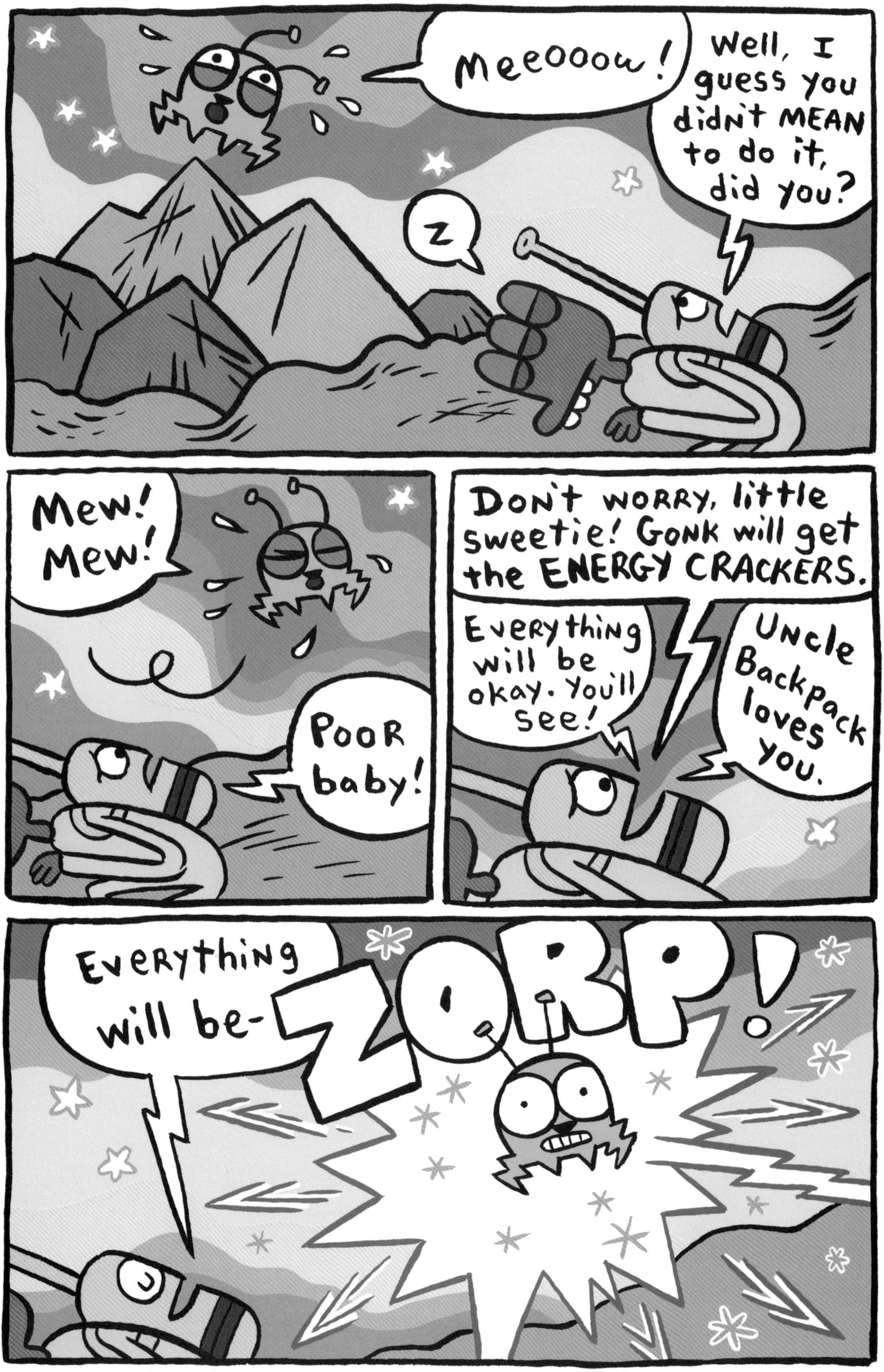
Meeoooow!
Well, I guess you didn't MEAN to do it, did you?
Z
Mew! Mew!
POOR baby!
Don't worry, little sweetie! GONK will get the ENERGY CRACKERS.
Everything will be okay. You'll see!
Uncle Backpack loves you.
Everything will be-
ZORP!

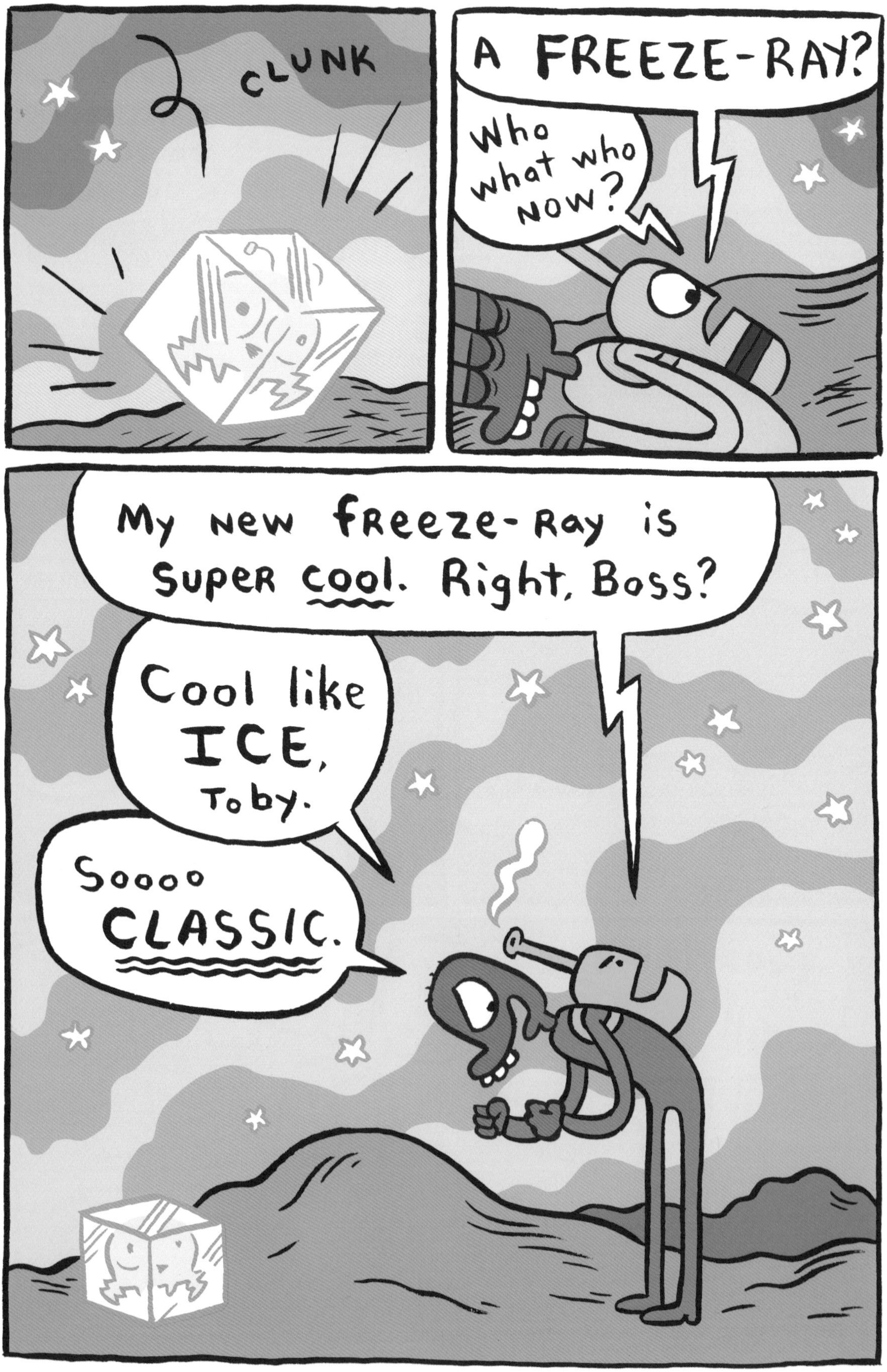
CLUNK
A FREEZE-RAY?
Who what who NOW?
My new freeze-Ray is super cool. Right, Boss?
Cool like ICE, Toby.
Soooo CLASSIC.

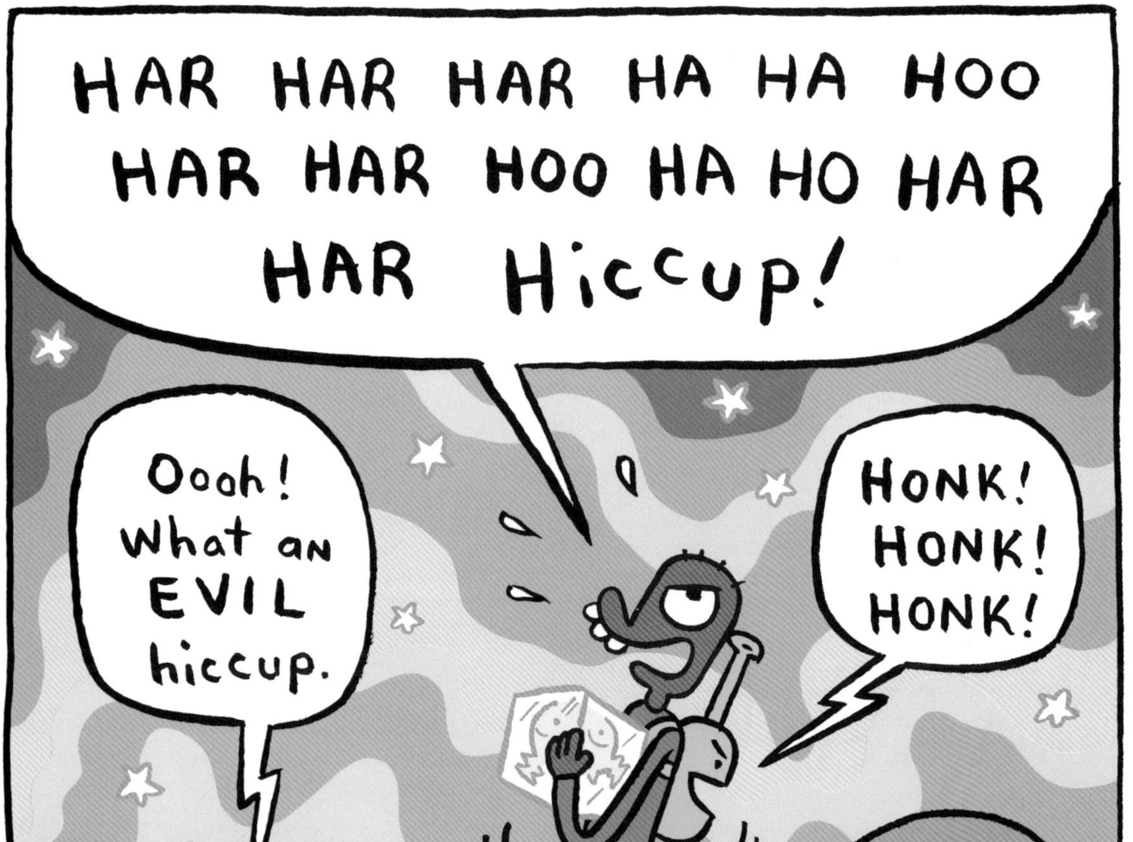
HAR HAR HAR HA HA HOO HAR HAR HOO HA HO HAR HAR Hiccup!
Oooh! What an EVIL hiccup.
HONK! HONK! HONK!

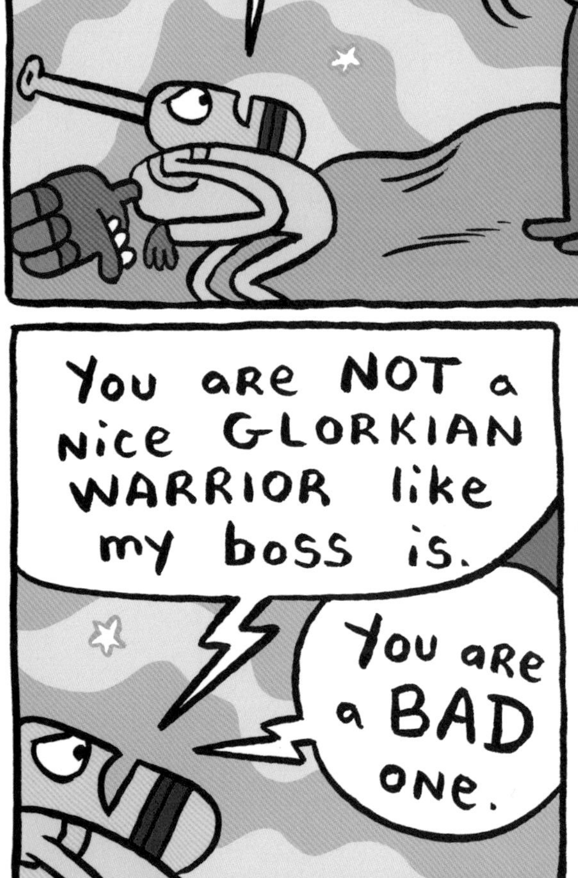
You are NOT a nice GLORKIAN WARRIOR like my boss is.
You are a BAD one.

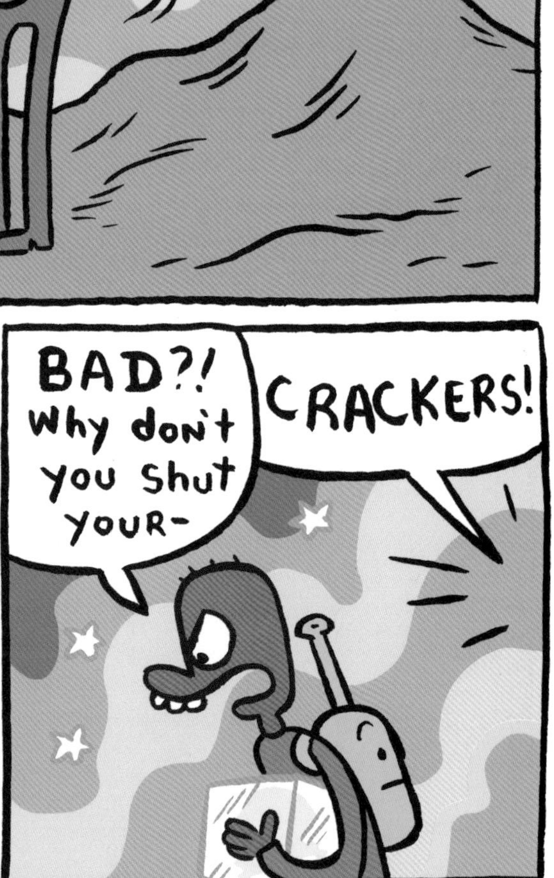
BAD?! Why don't you shut your-
CRACKERS!

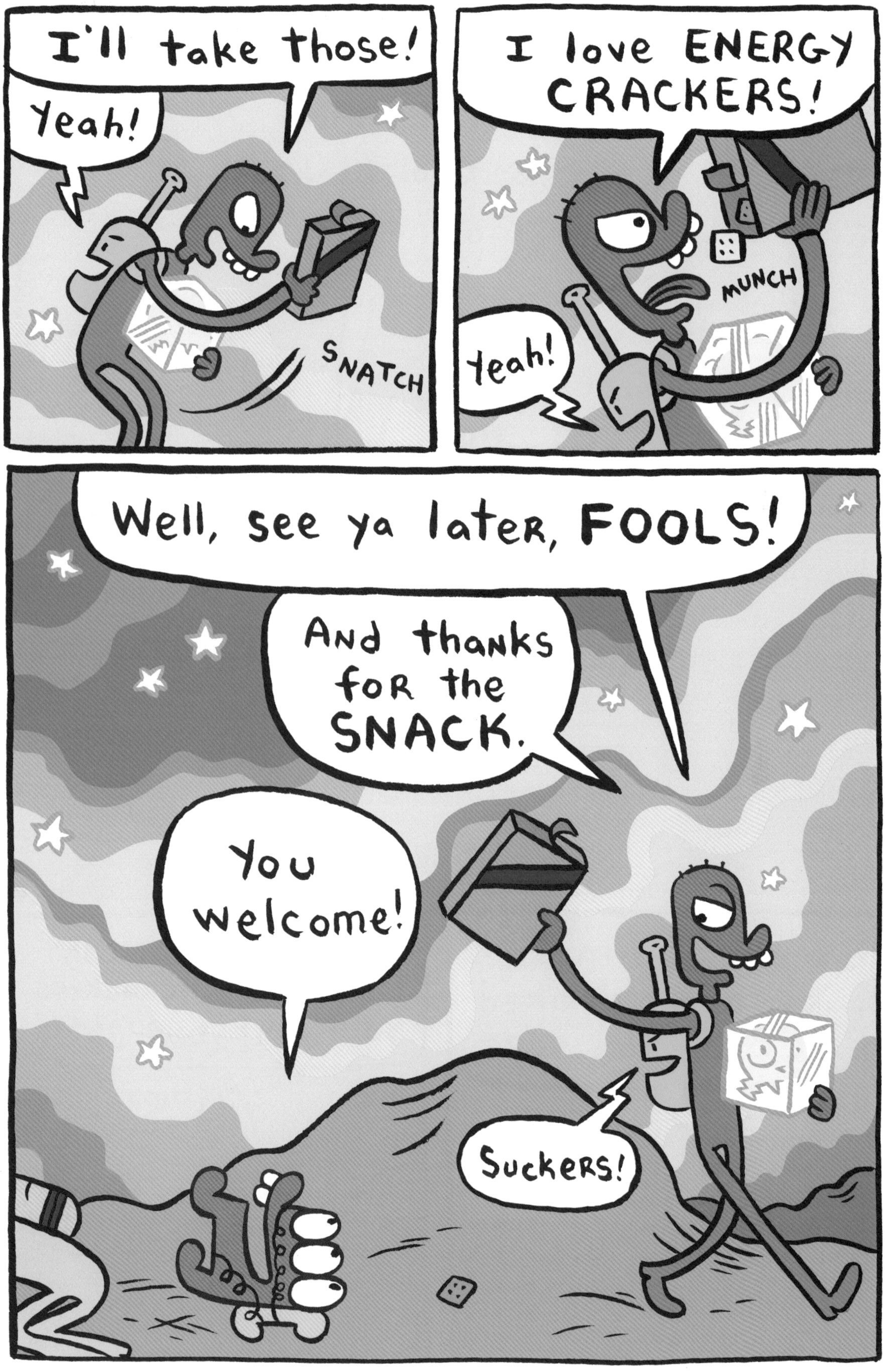

I'll take those!
Yeah!
SNATCH
I love ENERGY CRACKERS!
MUNCH
Yeah!
Well, see ya later, FOOLS!
And thanks for the SNACK.
You welcome!
Suckers!

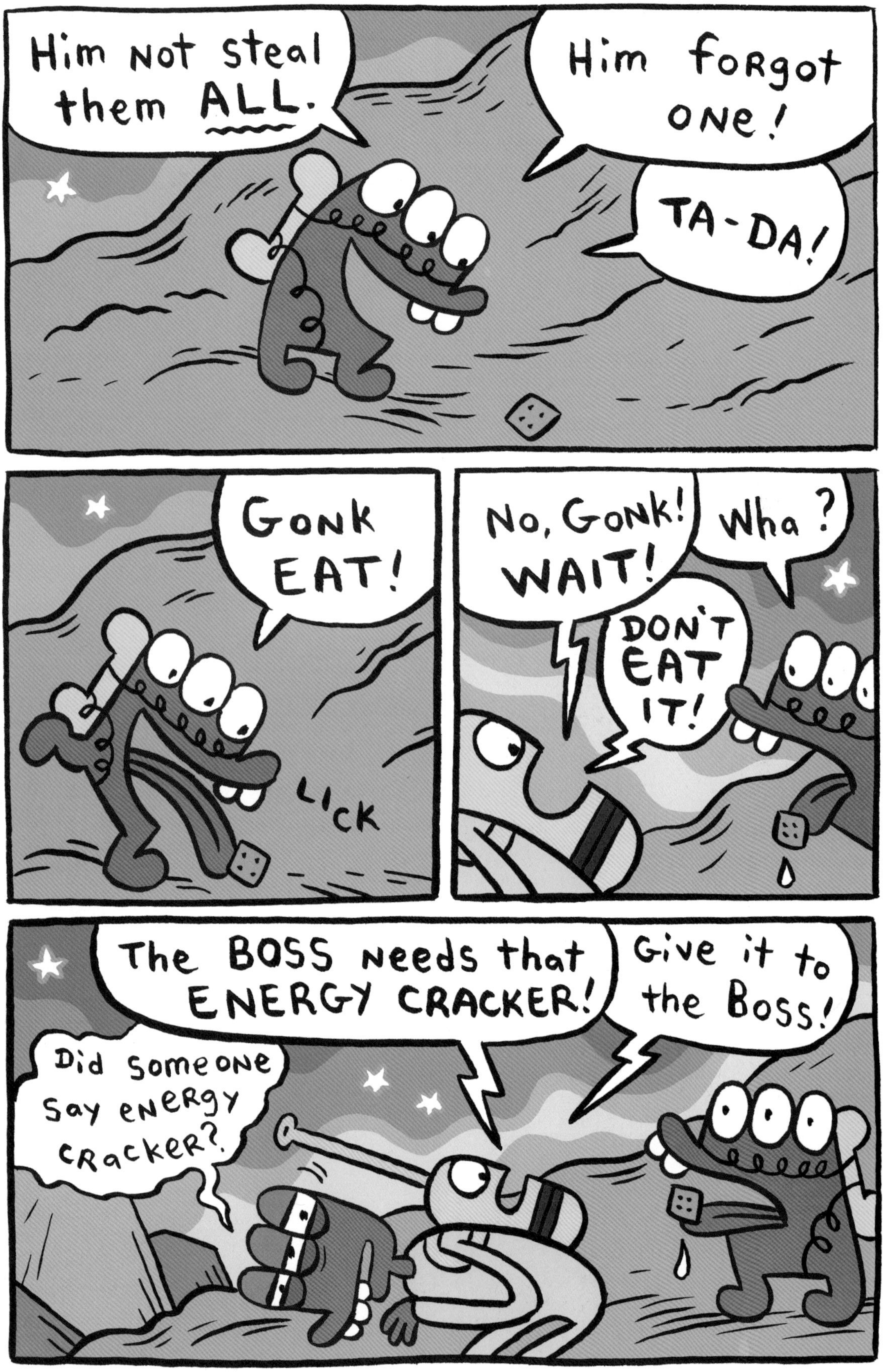
Him not steal them ALL.
Him forgot one!
TA-DA!
Gonk EAT!
LICK
No, Gonk! WAIT!
DON'T EAT IT!
Wha?
The BOSS needs that ENERGY CRACKER!
Give it to the Boss!
Did someone say energy cracker?

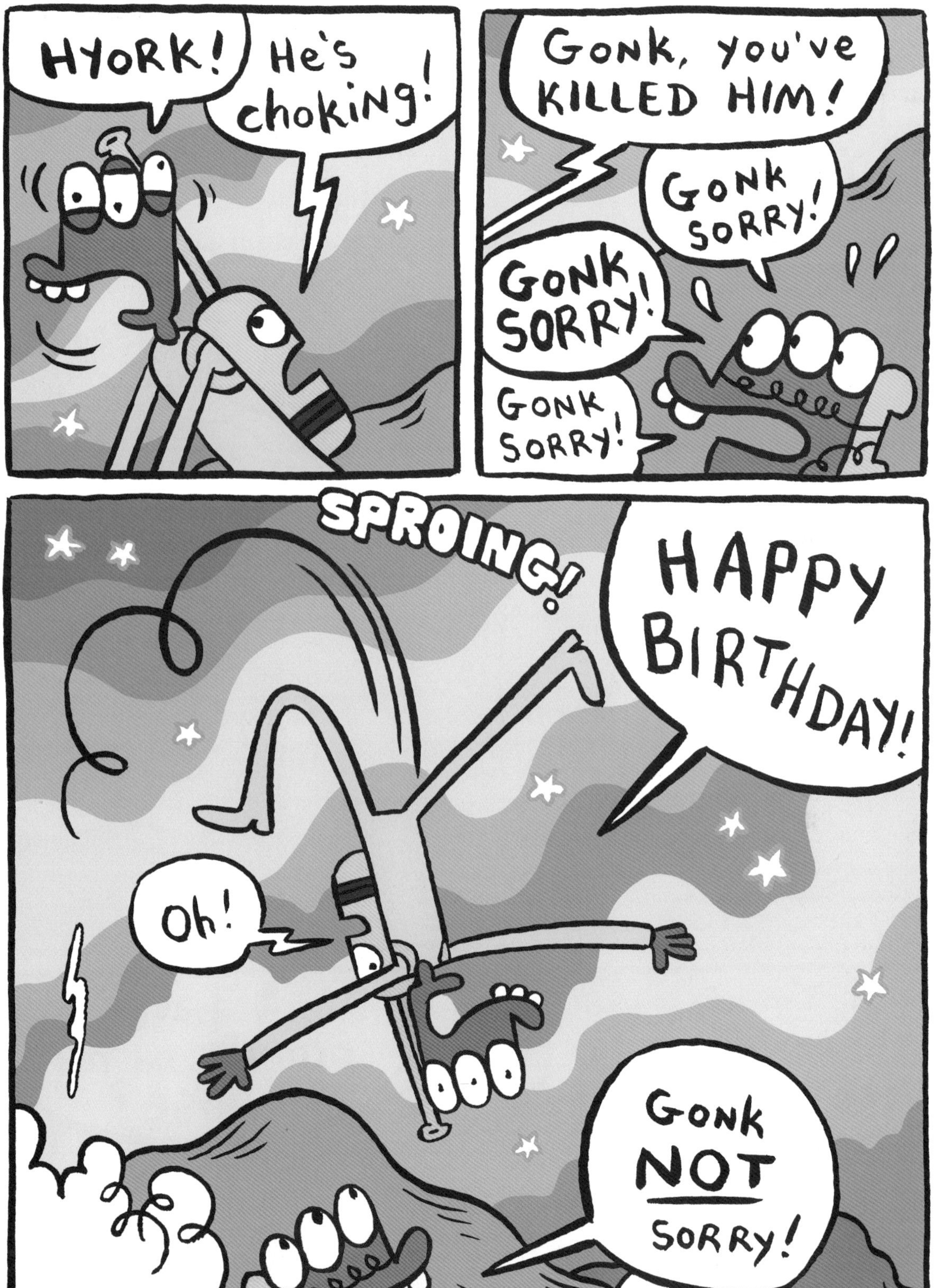
HYORK!
He's choking!
Gonk, you've KILLED HIM!
GONK SORRY!
GONK SORRY!
GONK SORRY!
SPROING!
HAPPY BIRTHDAY!
Oh!
Gonk NOT SORRY!
Yay!

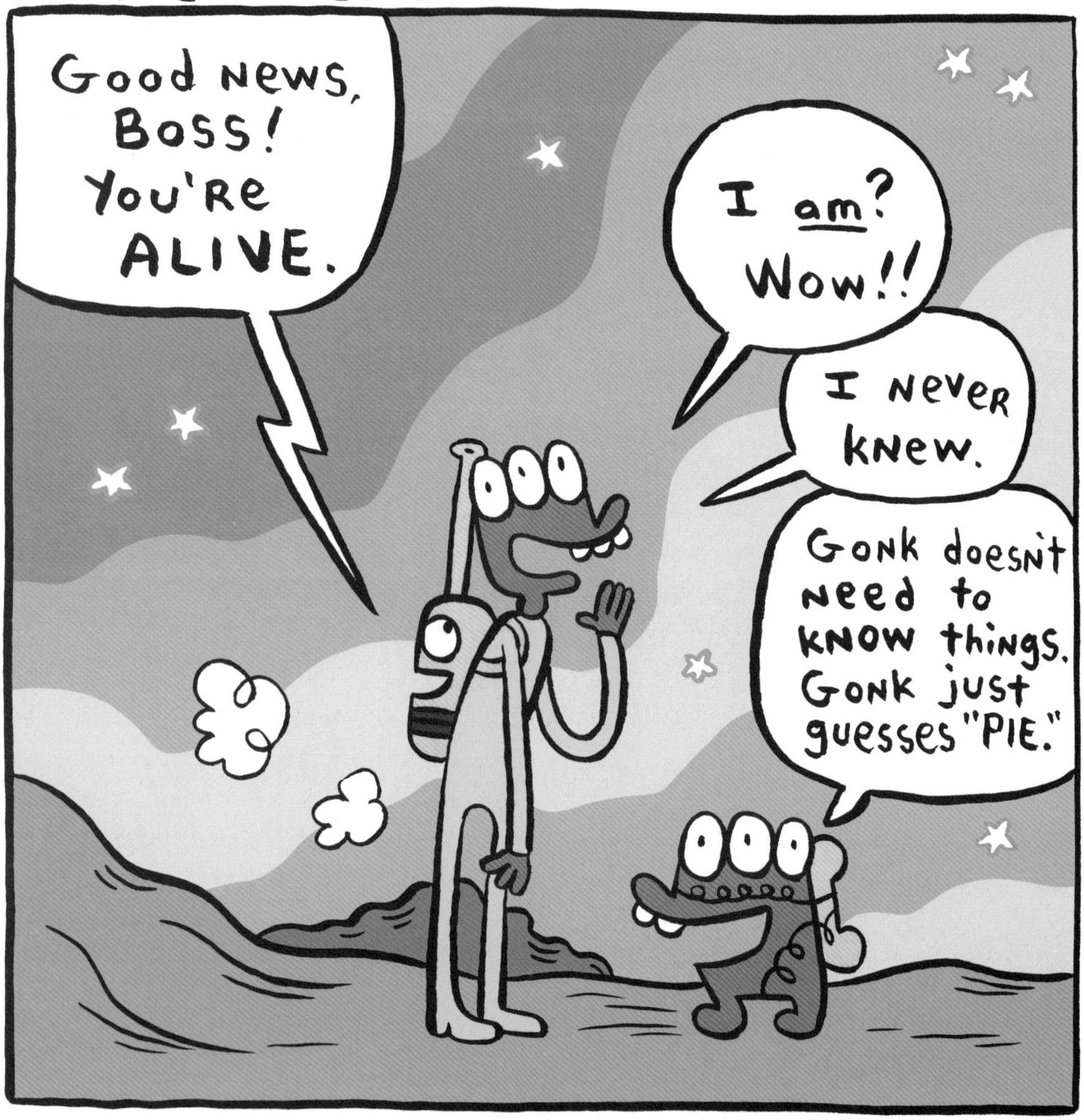
Good news, Boss! You're ALIVE.
I am? Wow!!
I never knew.
Gonk doesn't need to know things. Gonk just guesses "PIE."

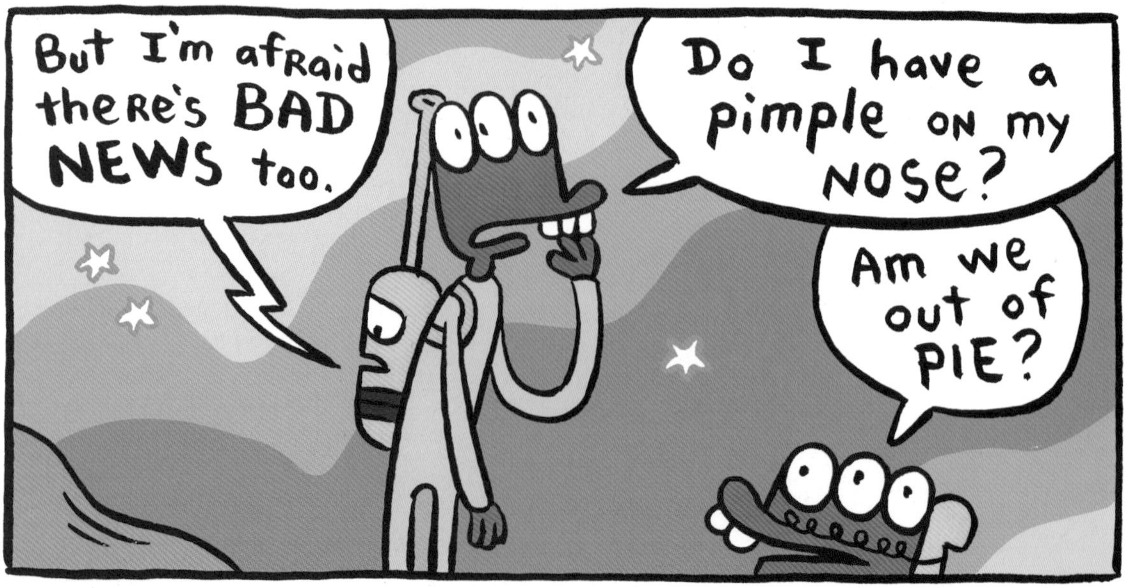
But I'm afraid there's BAD NEWS too.
Do I have a pimple on my nose?
Am we out of PIE?

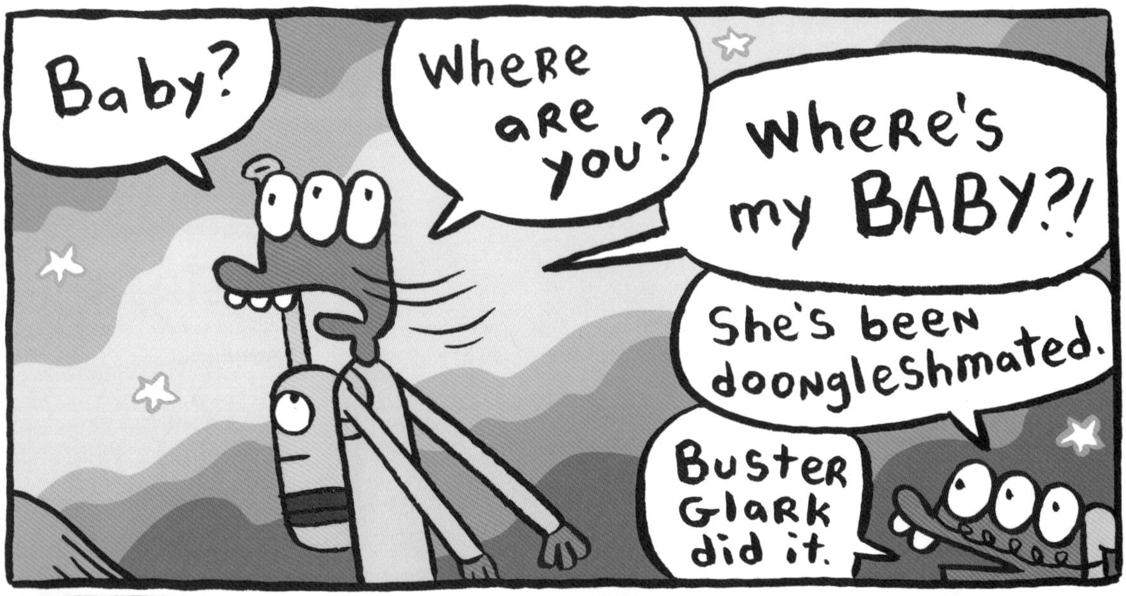
Baby?
Where are you?
Where's my BABY?!
She's been doongleshmated.
Buster Glark did it.

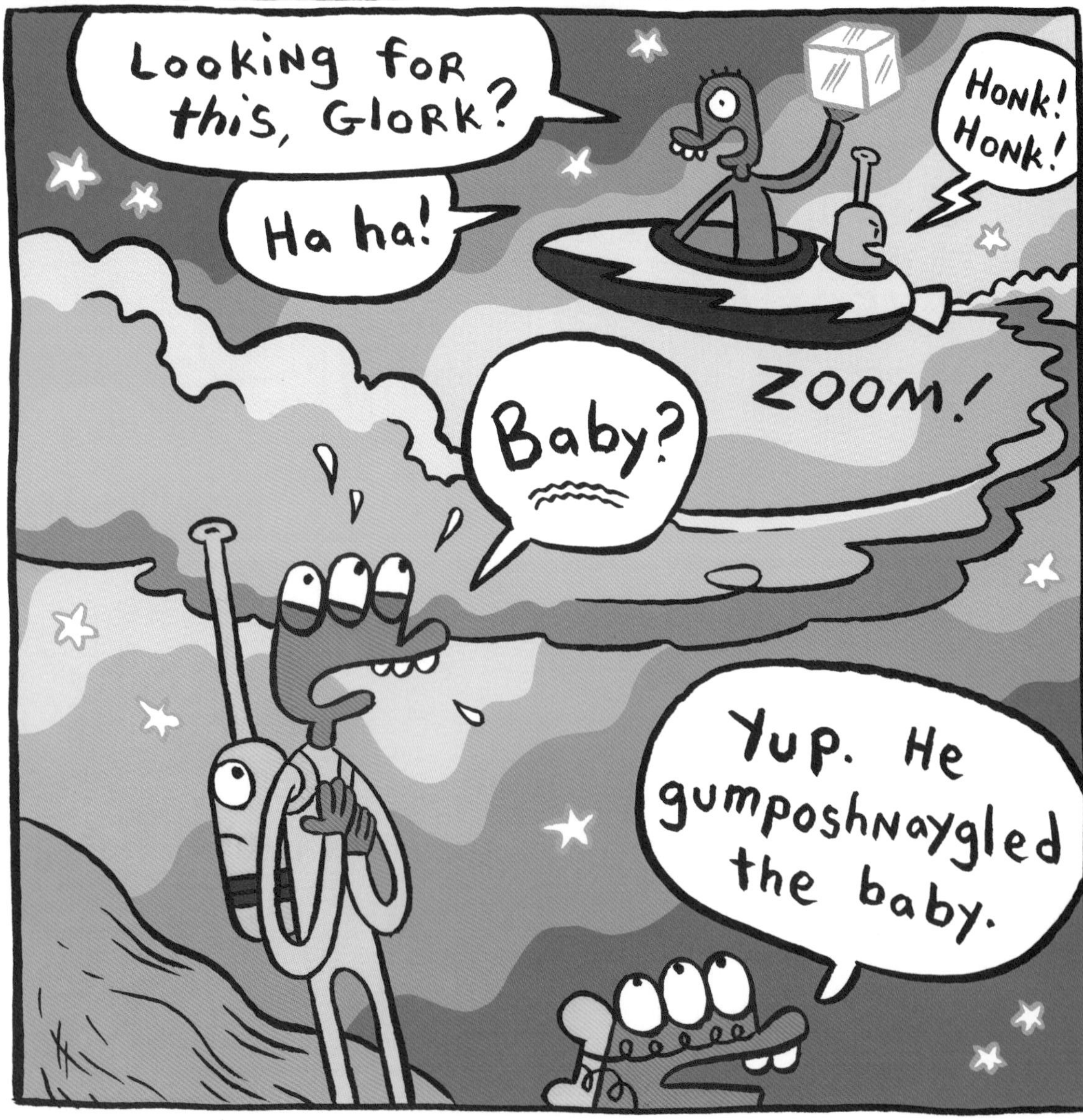
Looking for this, Glork?
Ha ha!
Honk! Honk!
ZOOM!
Baby?
Yup. He gumposhnaygled the baby.

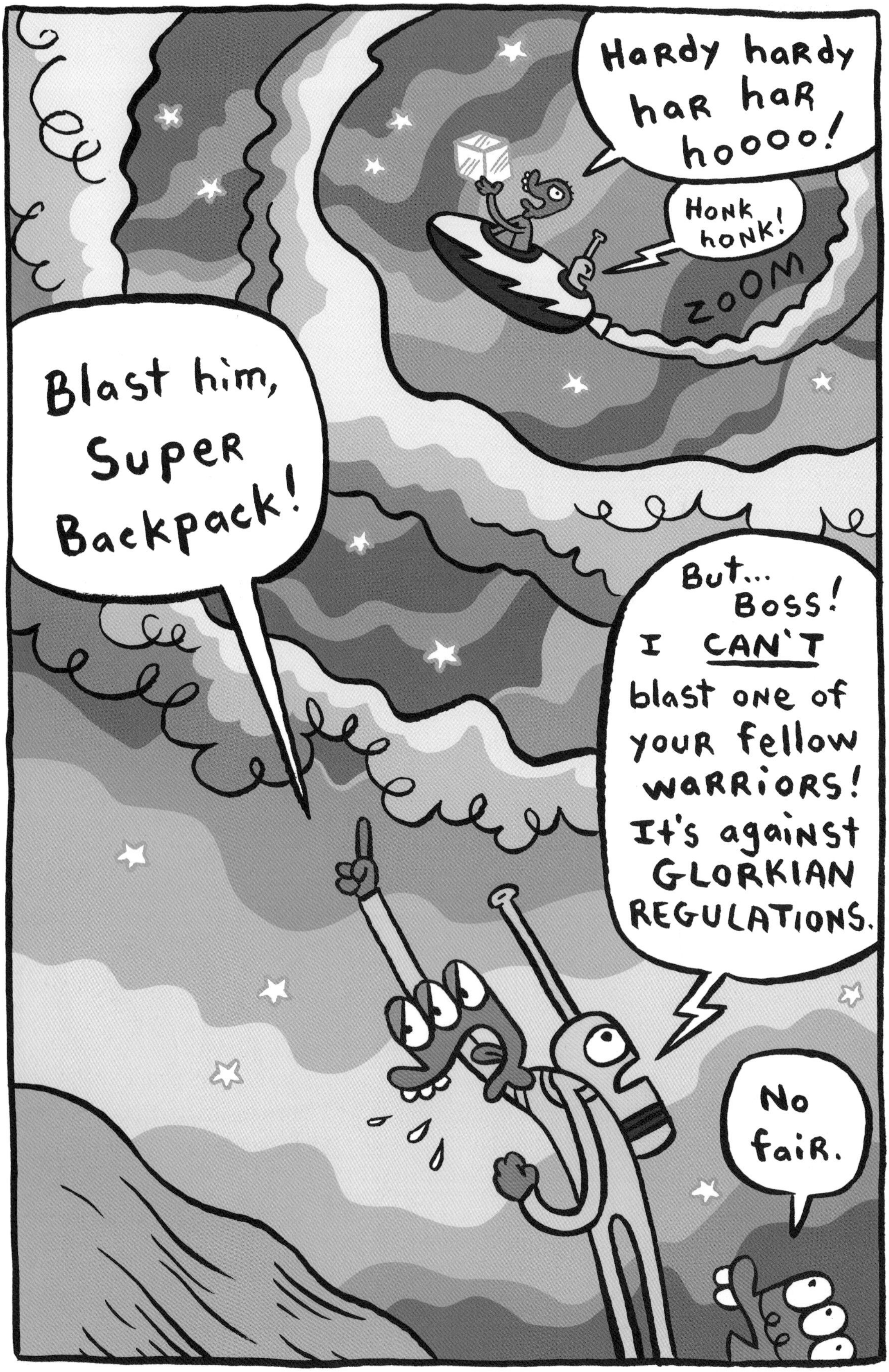
Hardy hardy har har hoooo!
HONK honk!
ZOOM
Blast him, Super Backpack!
But... Boss! I CAN'T blast one of your fellow warriors! It's against GLORKIAN REGULATIONS.
No fair.

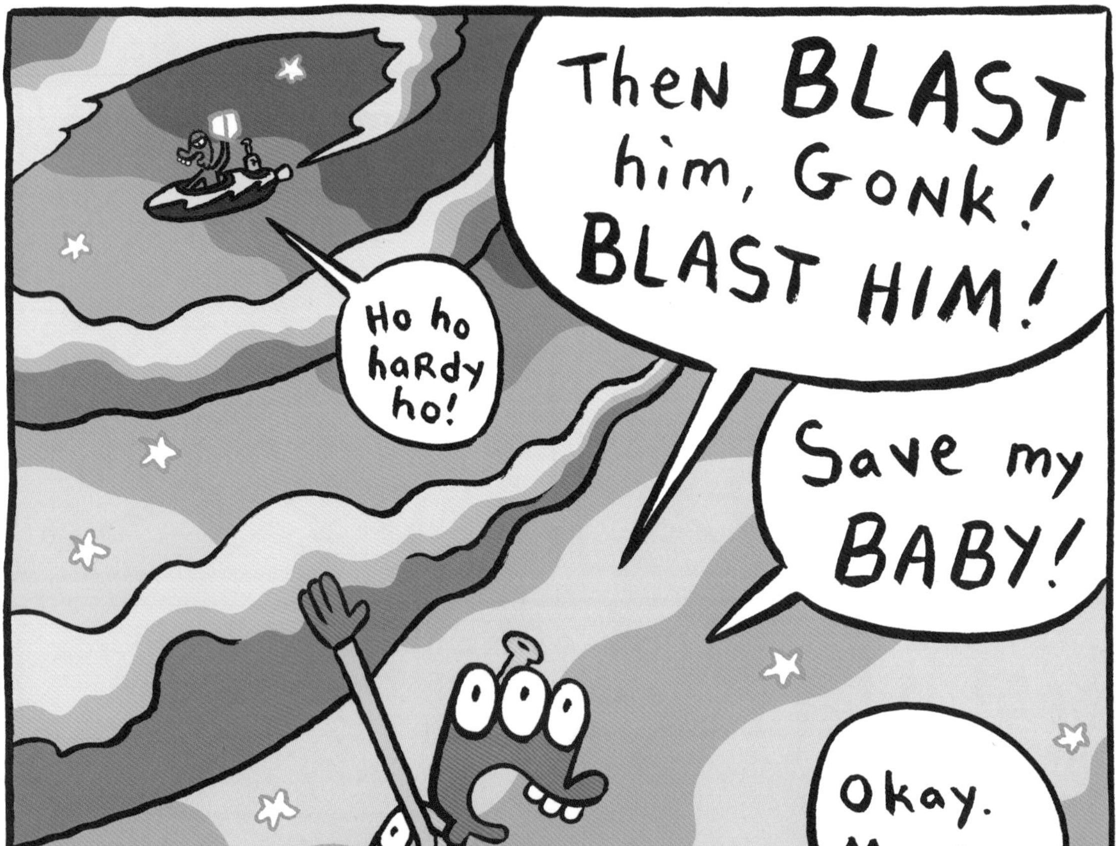
Then BLAST him, GONK! BLAST HIM!
Ho ho hardy ho!
Save my BABY!
Okay. Me try.
I don't know about this...

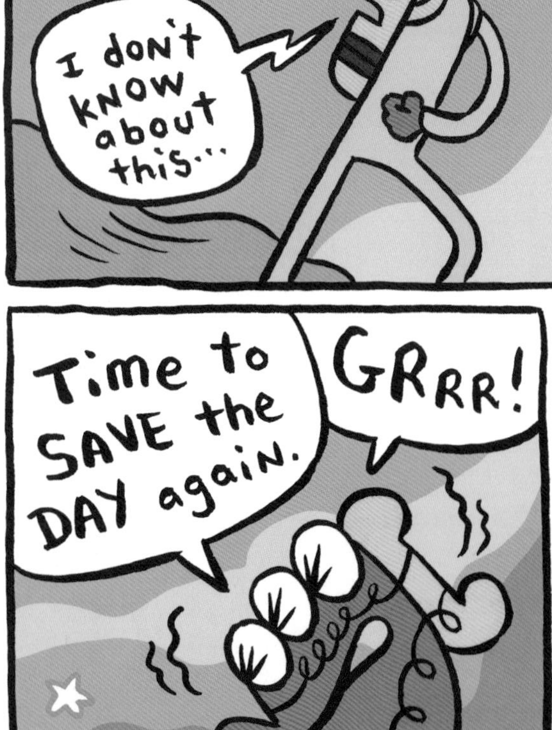
Time to SAVE the DAY again.
GRRR!

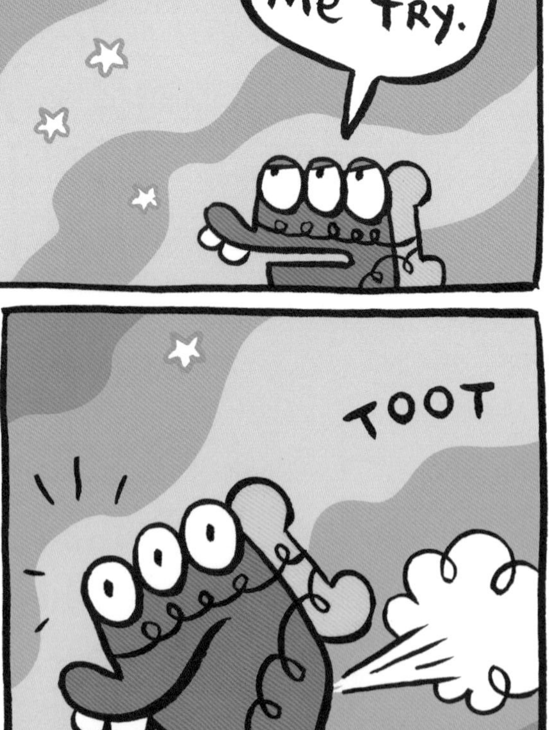
TOOT

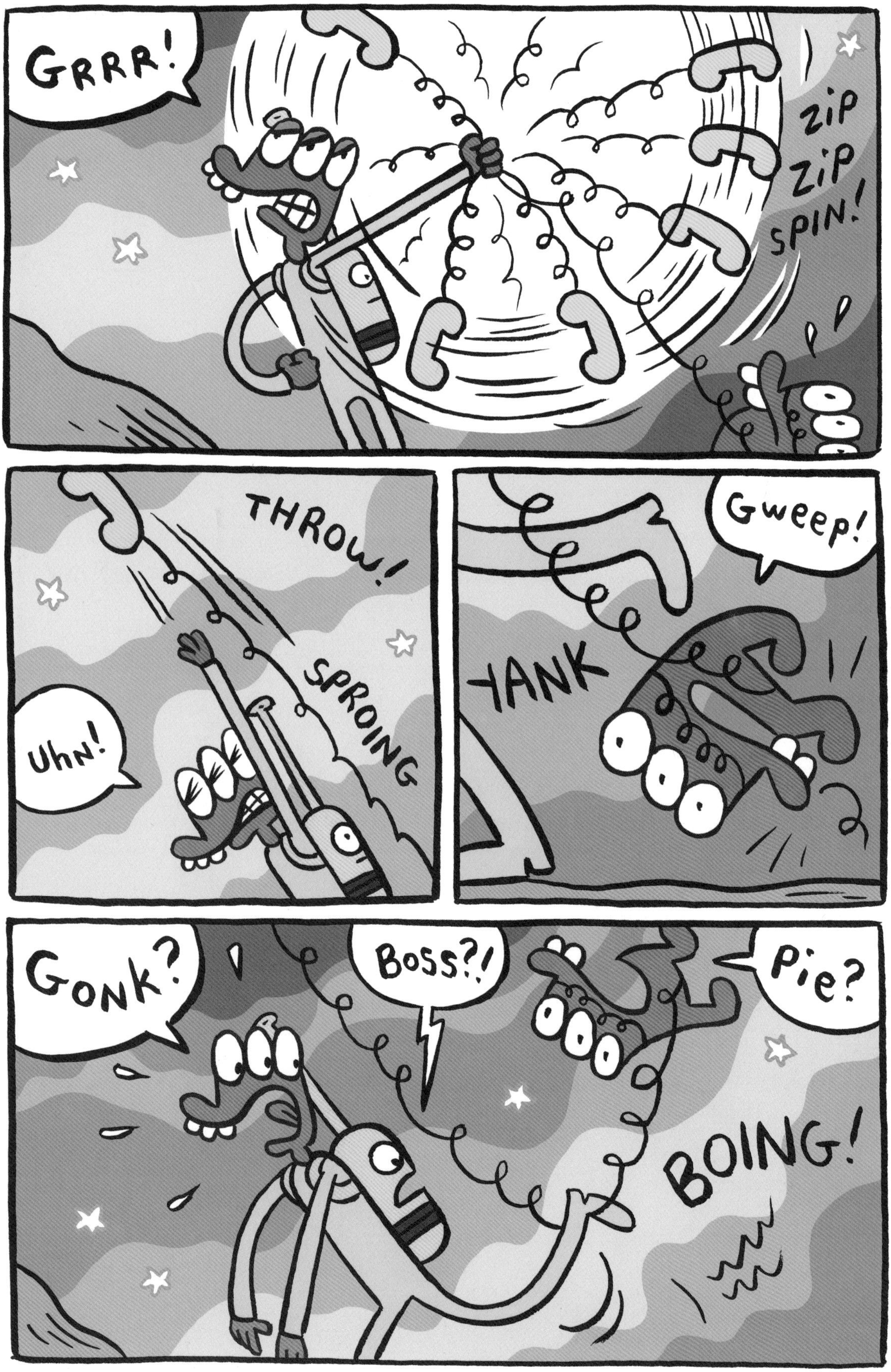
GRRR!
ZIP
ZIP
SPIN!
THROW!
SPROING
Uhn!
Gweep!
YANK
Gonk?
Boss?!
Pie?
BOING!

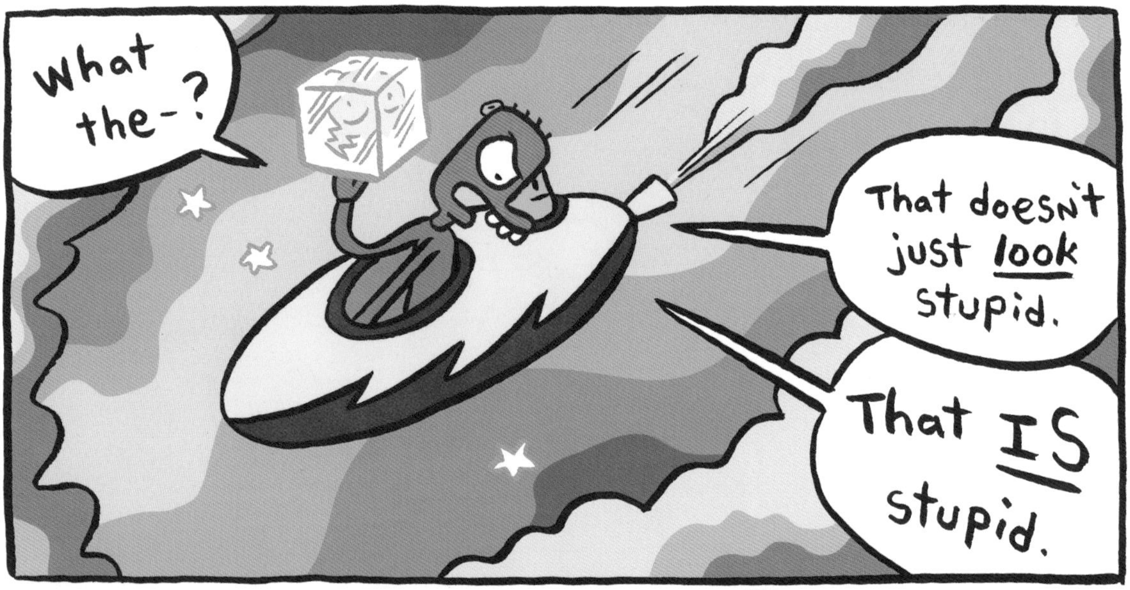
What the-?
That doesn't just look stupid.
That IS stupid.

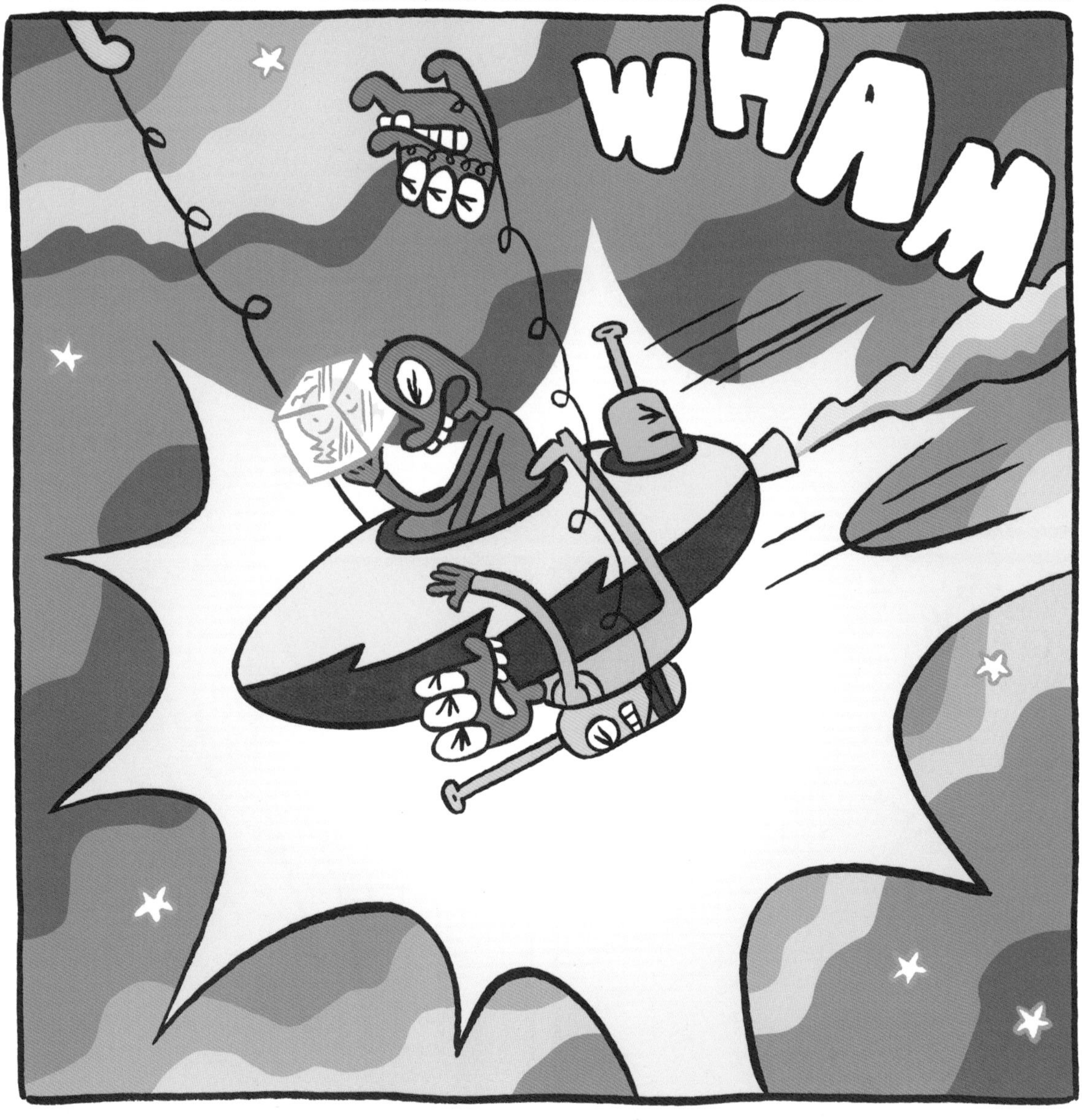
WHAM

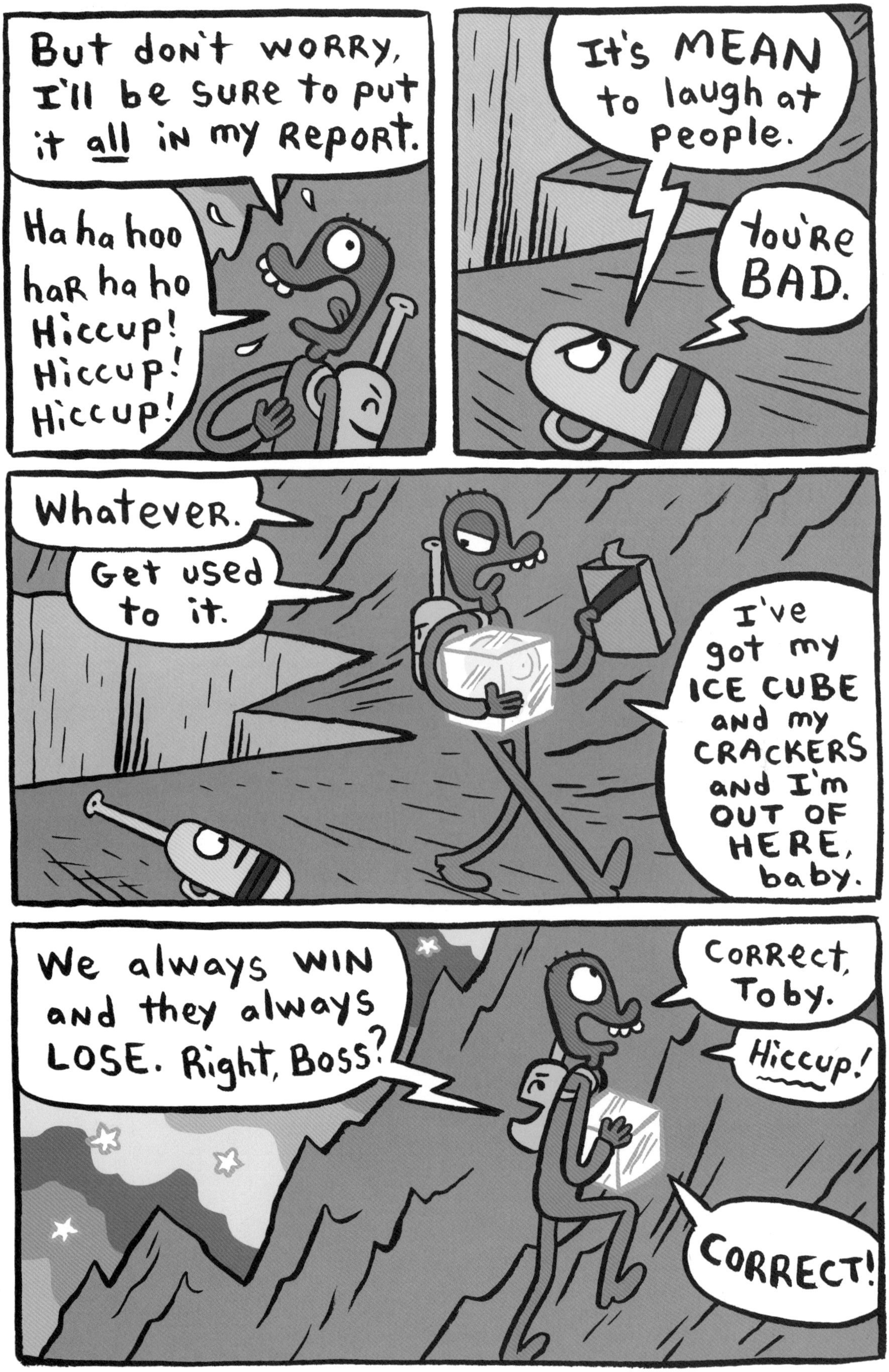
But don't worry, I'll be sure to put it all in my report.
Ha ha hoo har ha ho Hiccup! Hiccup! Hiccup!
It's MEAN to laugh at people.
You're BAD.
Whatever.
Get used to it.
I've got my ICE CUBE and my CRACKERS and I'm OUT OF HERE, baby.
We always WIN and they always LOSE. Right, Boss?
Correct, Toby.
Hiccup!
CORRECT!

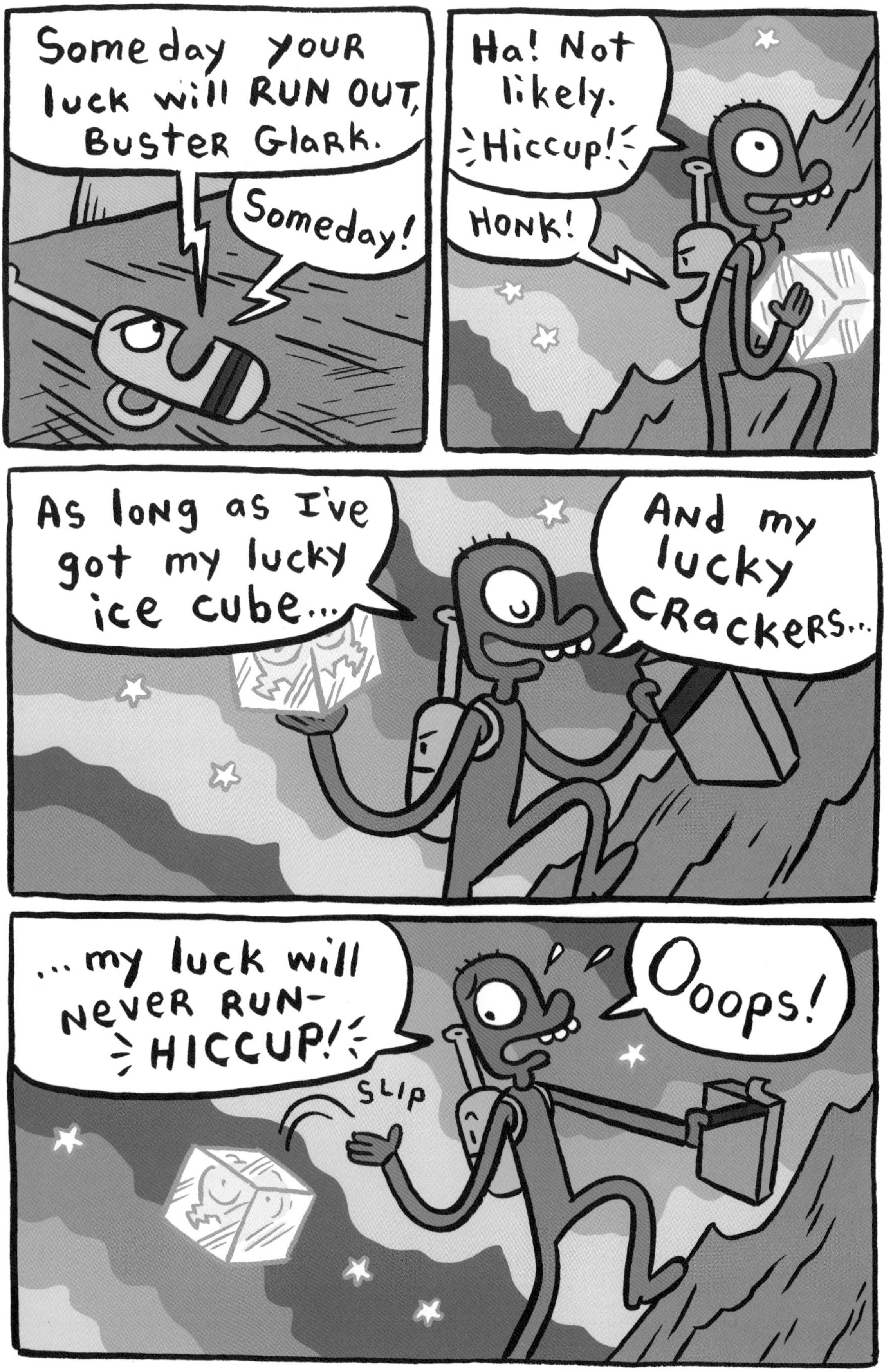
Someday YOUR luck will RUN OUT, Buster Glark.
Someday!
Ha! Not likely.
Hiccup!
HONK!
As long as I've got my lucky ice cube...
And my lucky crackers...
...my luck will never RUN-
HICCUP!
SLIP
Ooops!

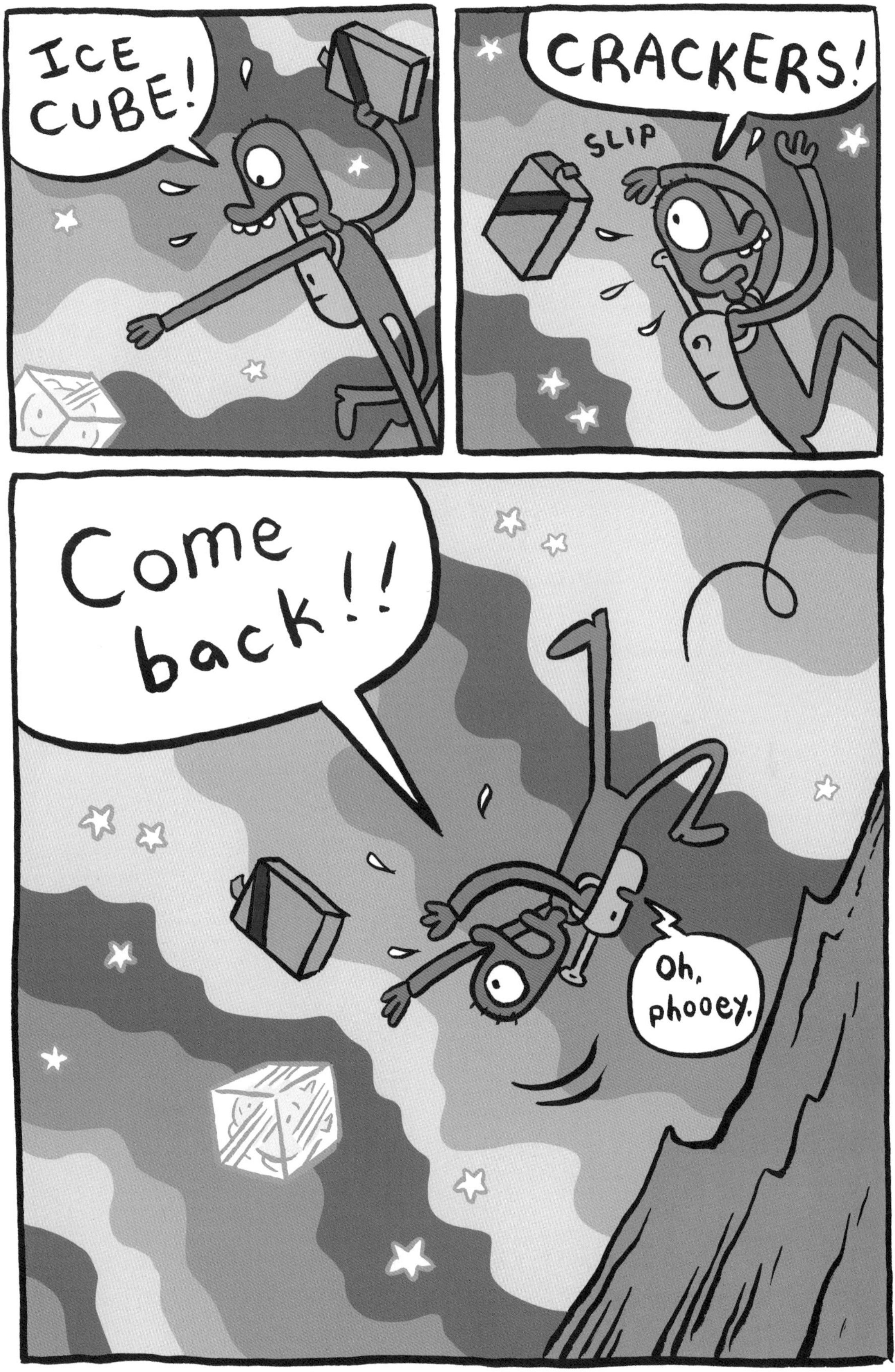
ICE CUBE!
CRACKERS!
SLIP
Come back!!
Oh, phooey.

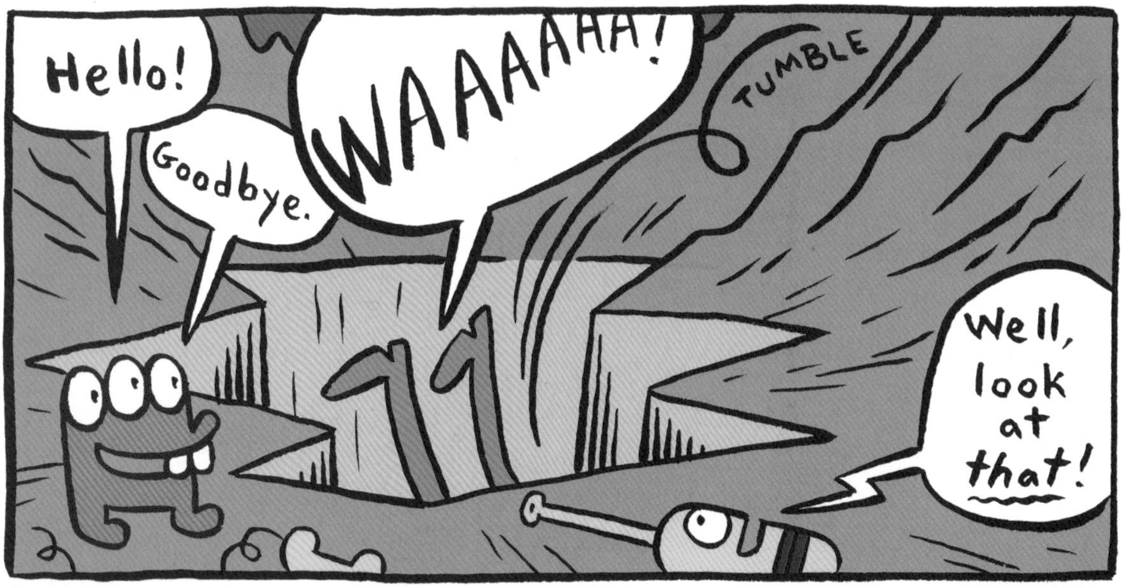
Hello!
Goodbye.
WAAAAAHA!
TUMBLE
Well, look at that!

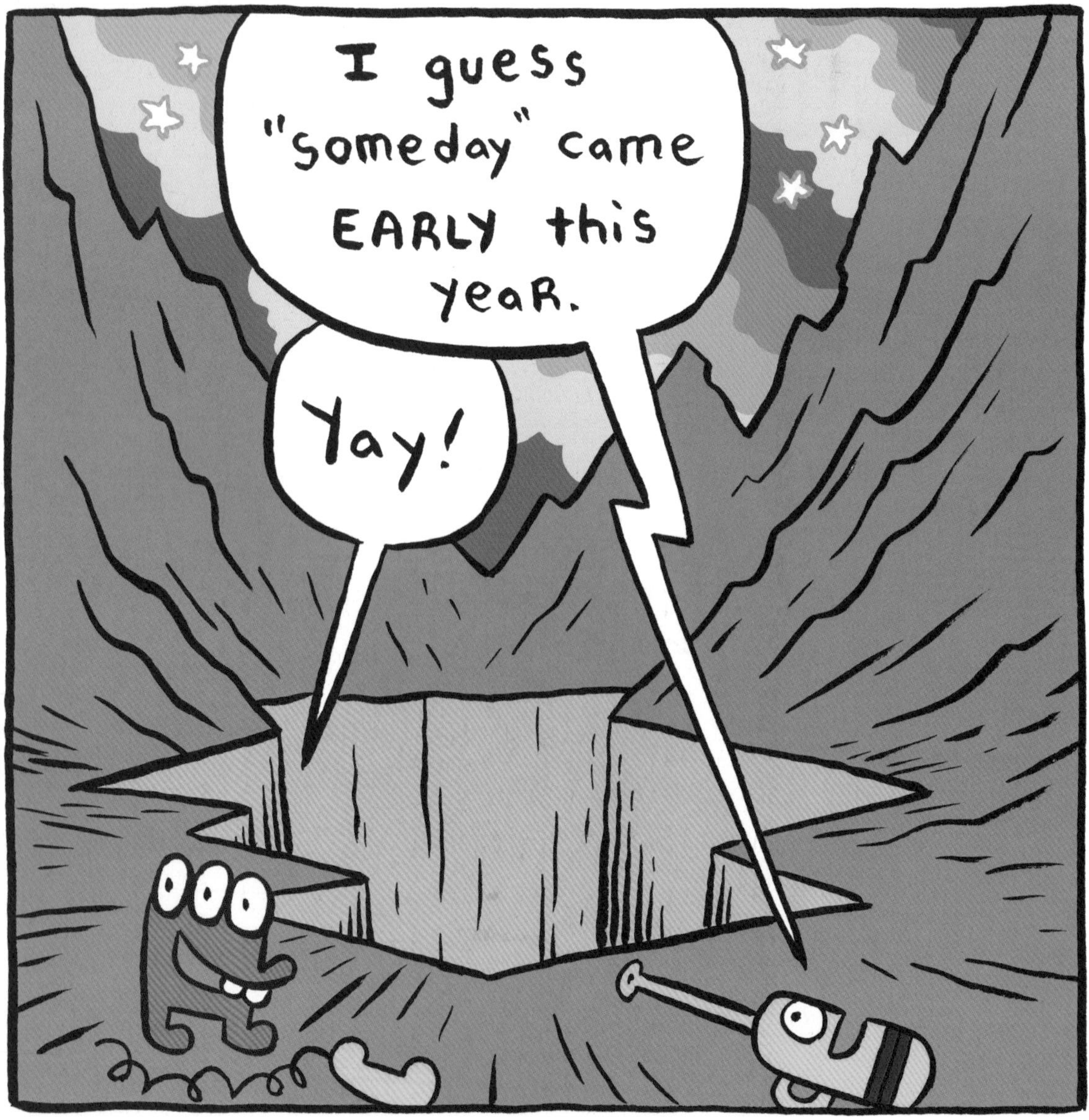
I guess "someday" came EARLY this year.
Yay!

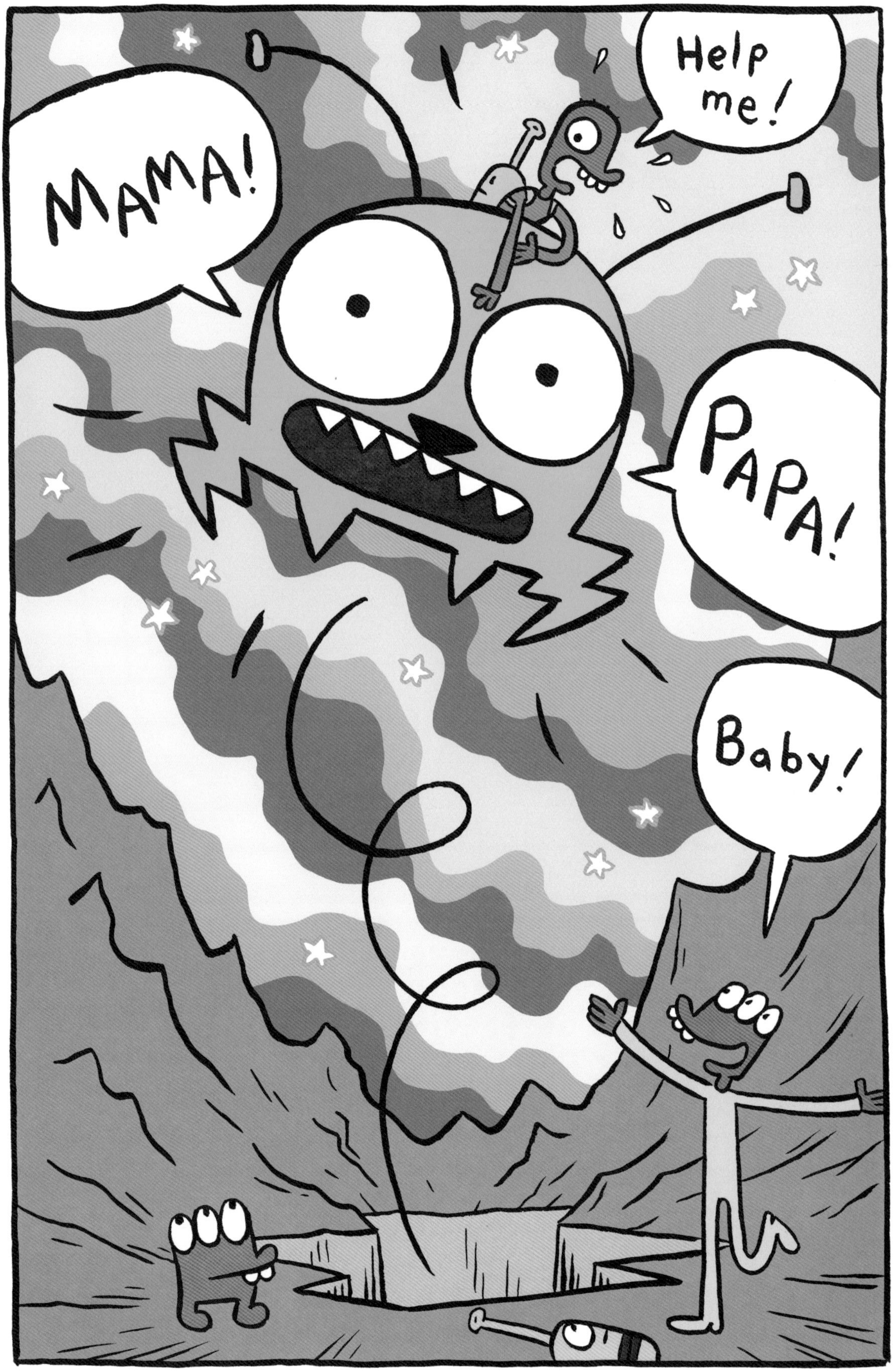
MAMA!
Help me!
PAPA!
Baby!

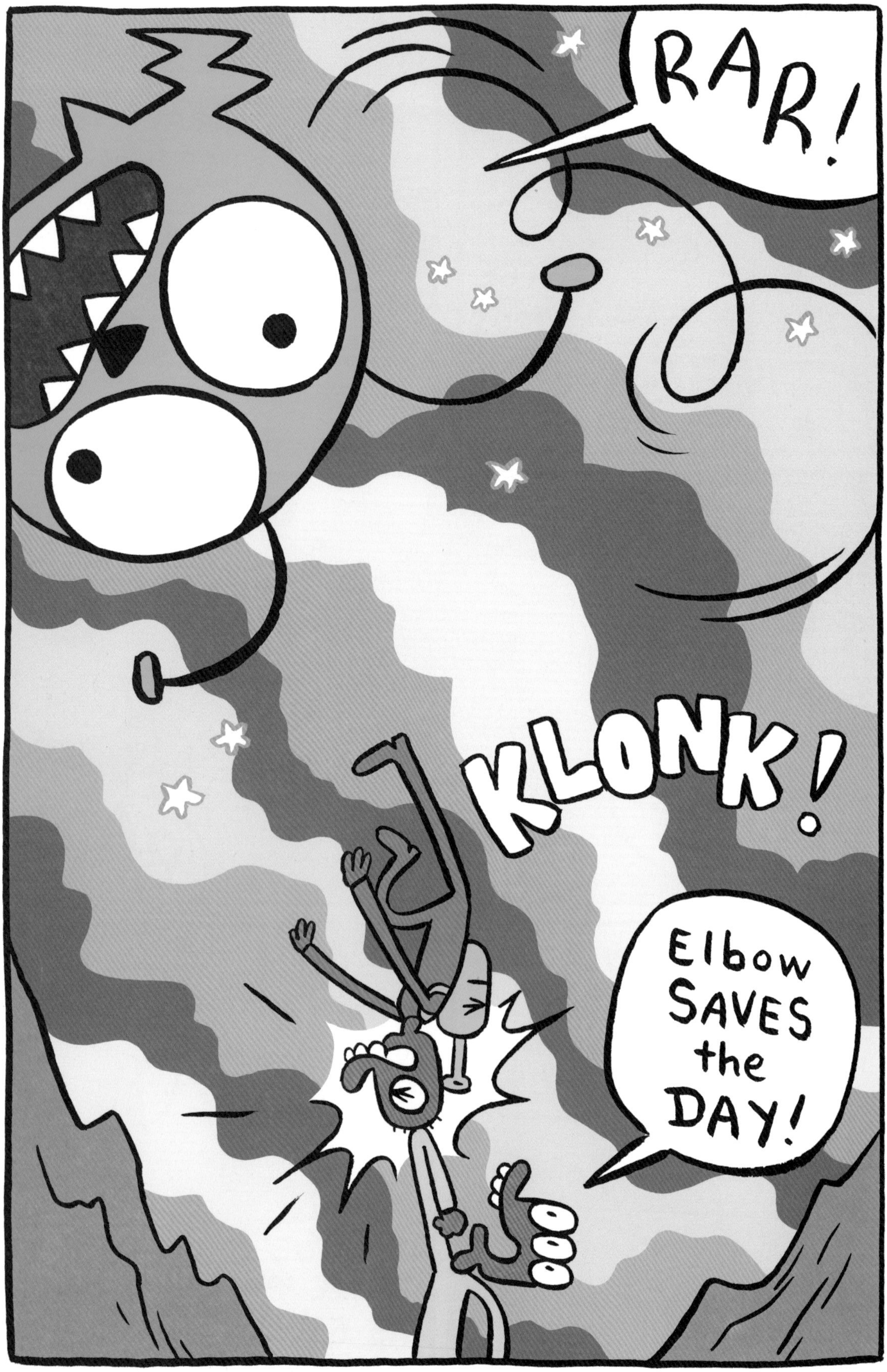
RAR!
KLONK!
Elbow SAVES the DAY!

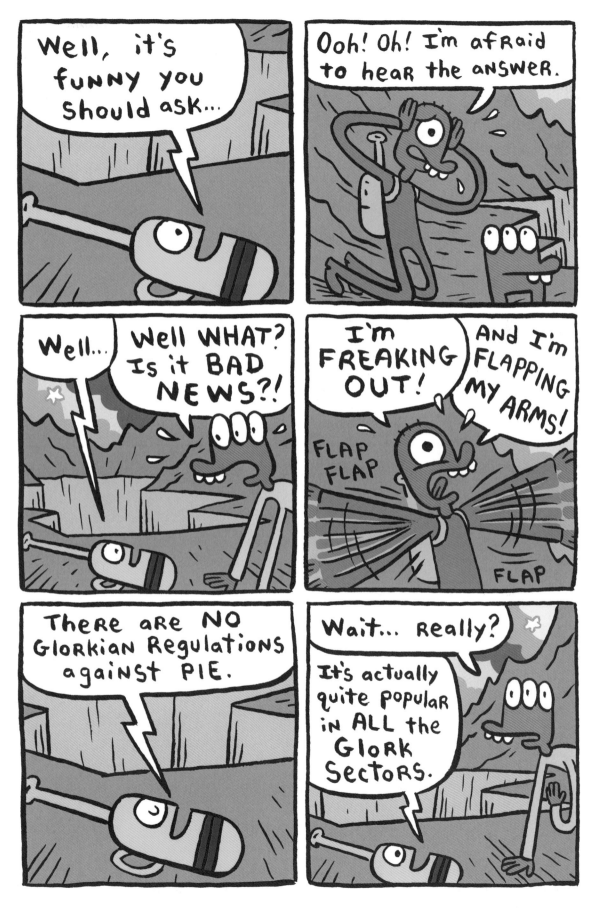

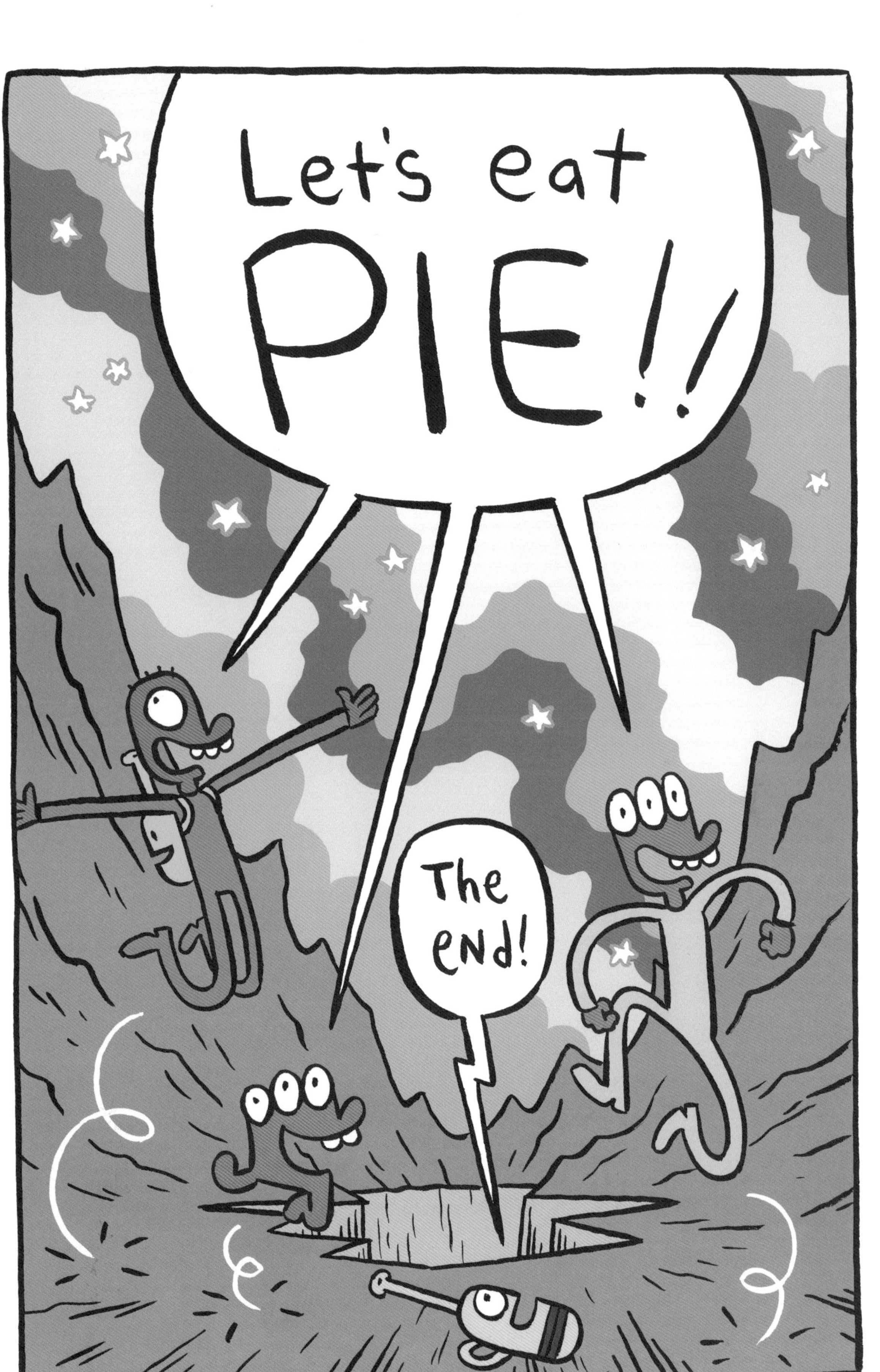
Let's eat PIE!!!
The end!

EPILOGUE

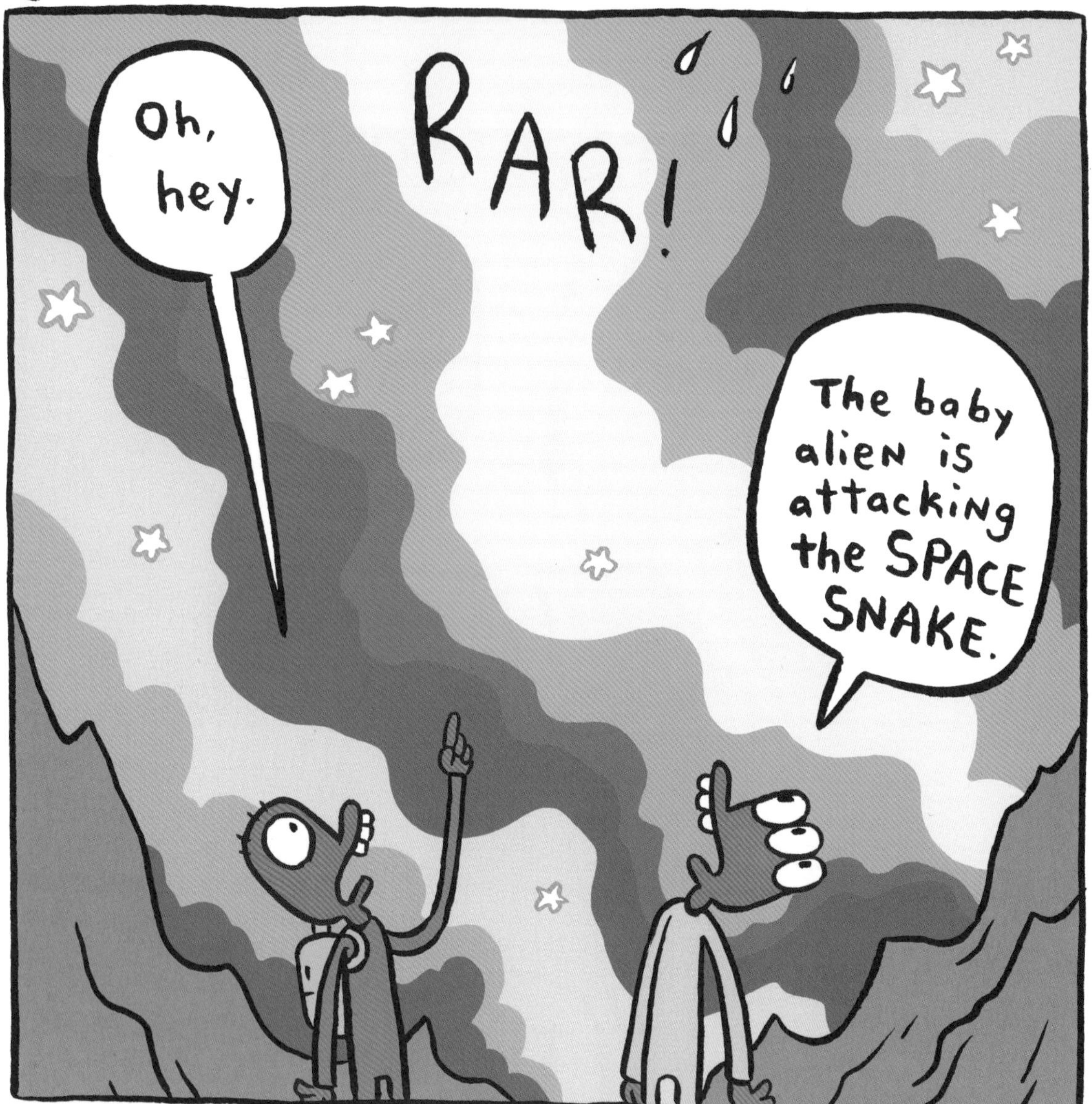
RAR!
Oh, hey.
The baby alien is attacking the SPACE SNAKE.

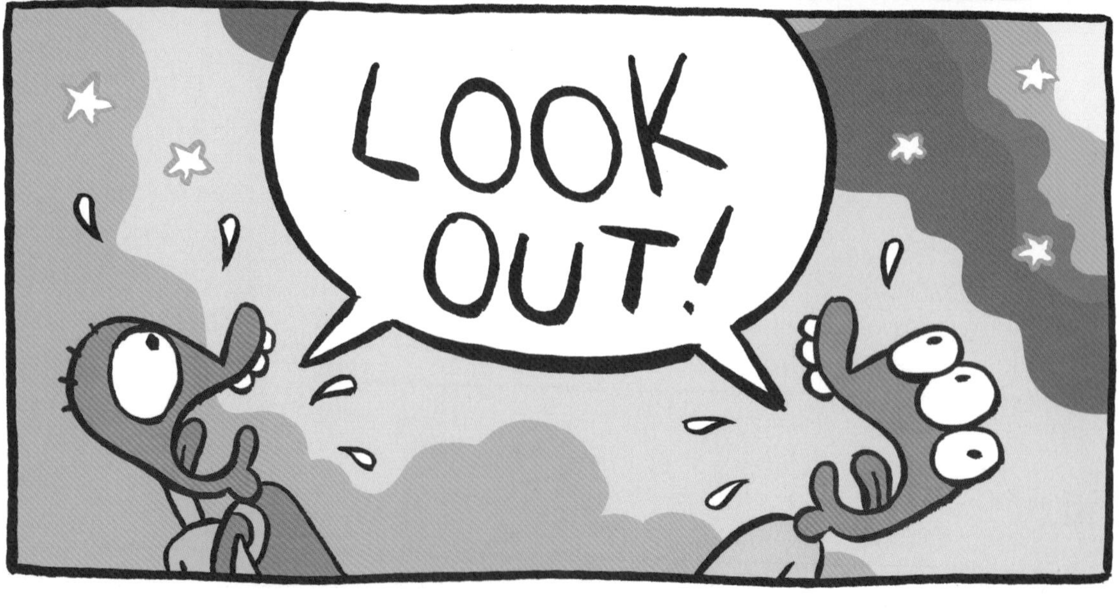
LOOK OUT!

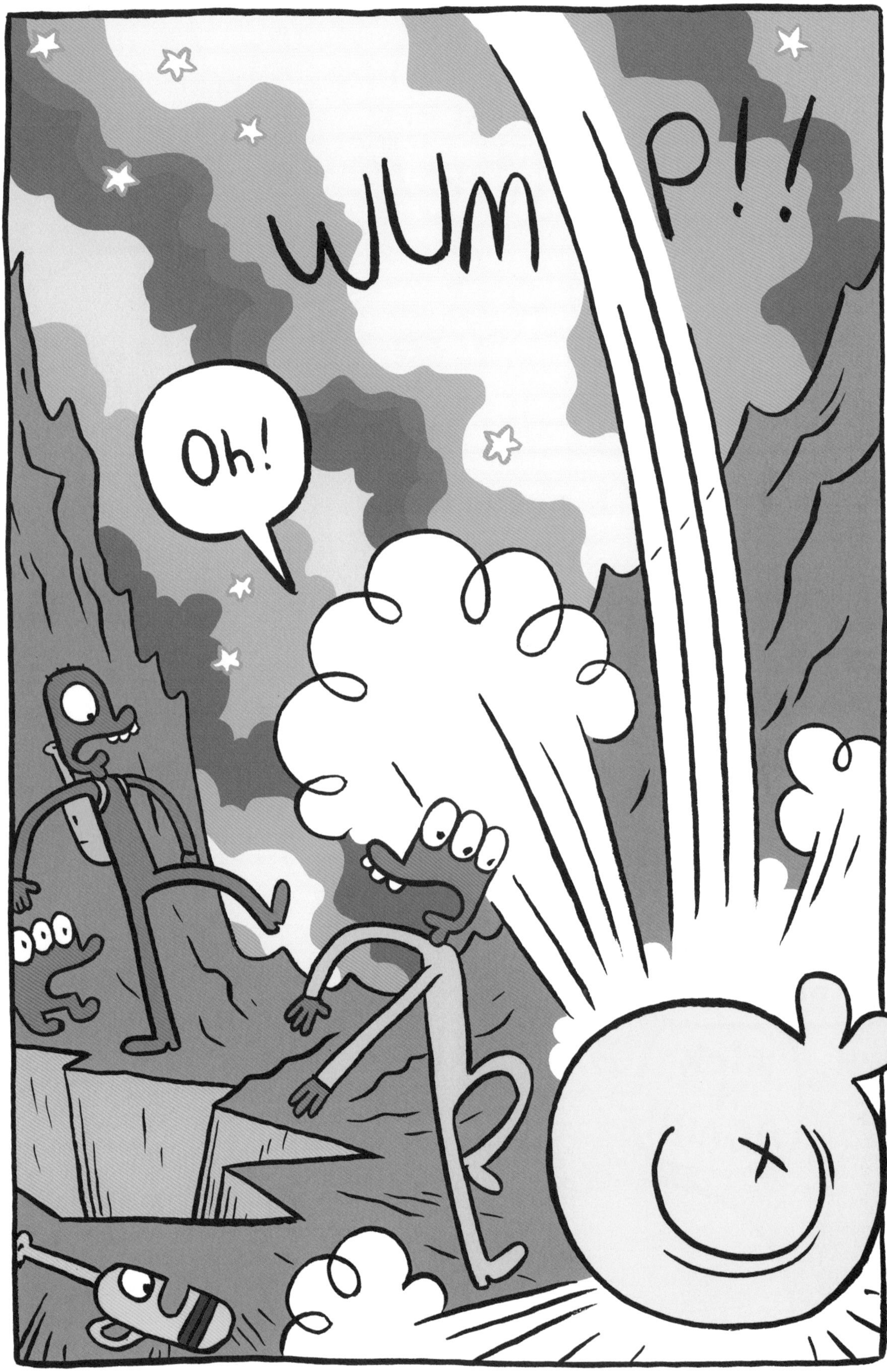
WUMP!!
Oh!

116

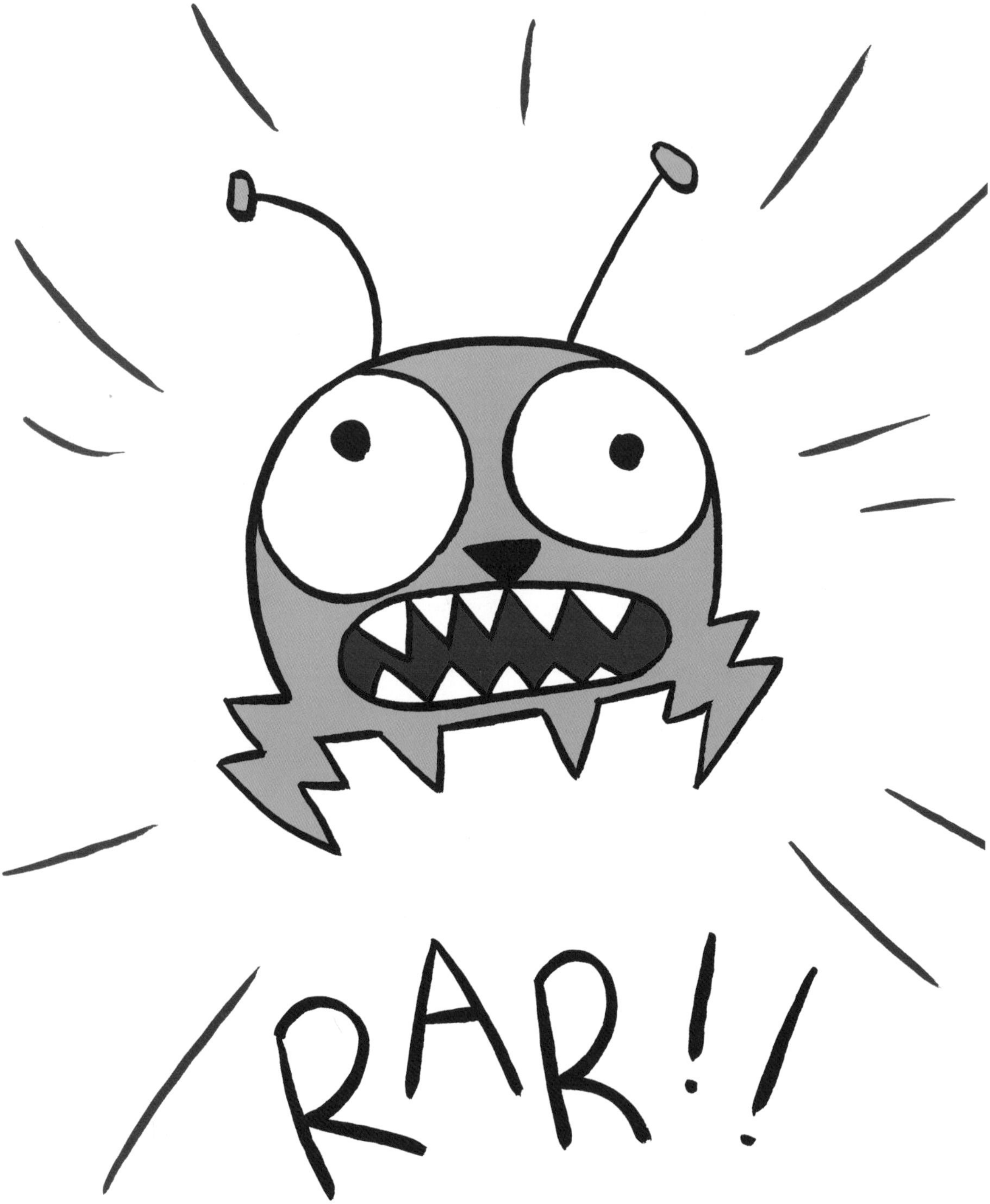
RAR!!

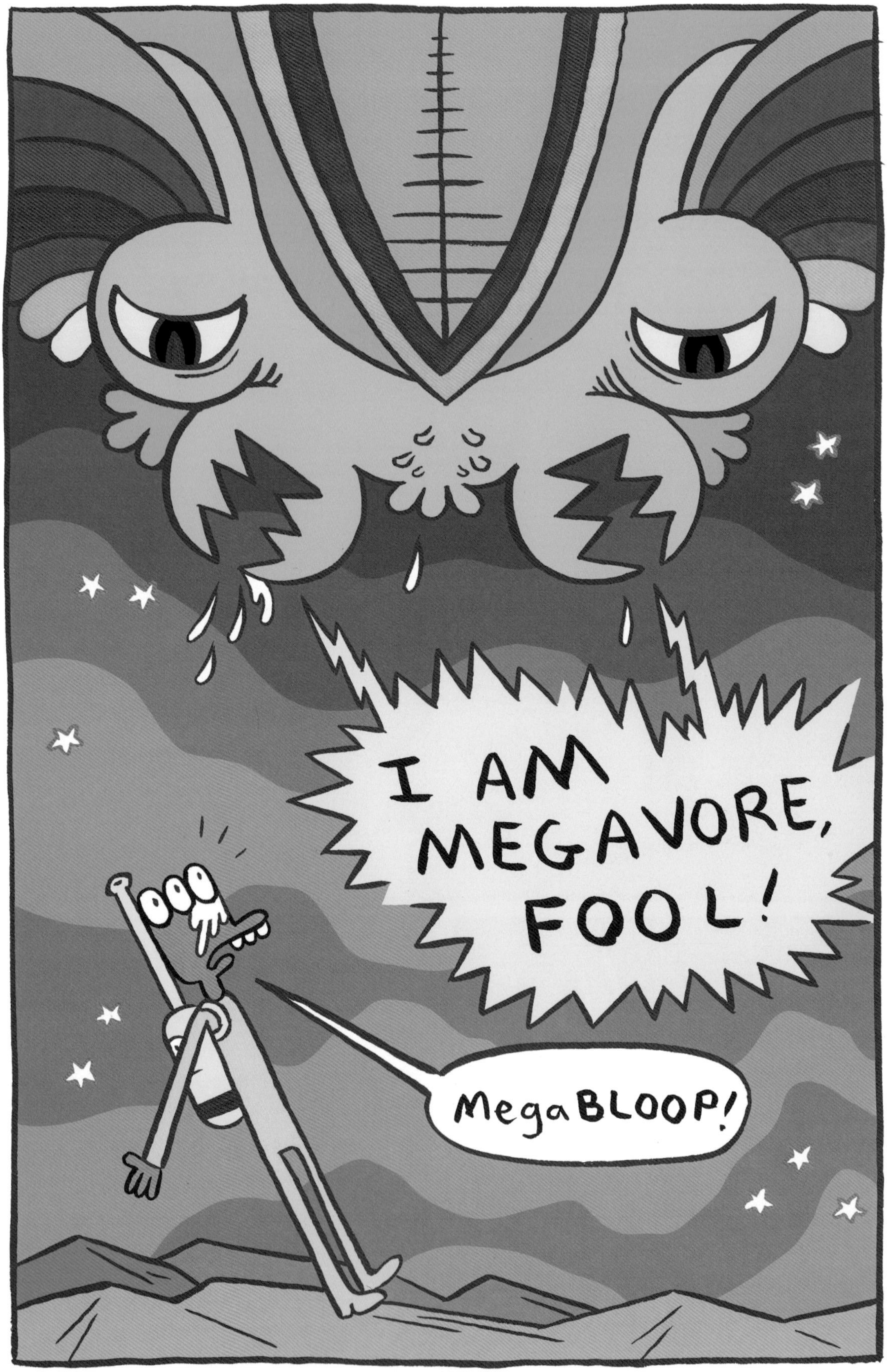
I AM MEGAVORE, FOOL!
MegaBLOOP!

AN AMAZING WATER STAIN THAT LOOKS EXACTLY LIKE THE REAL GLORKIAN WARRIOR, SORT OF.

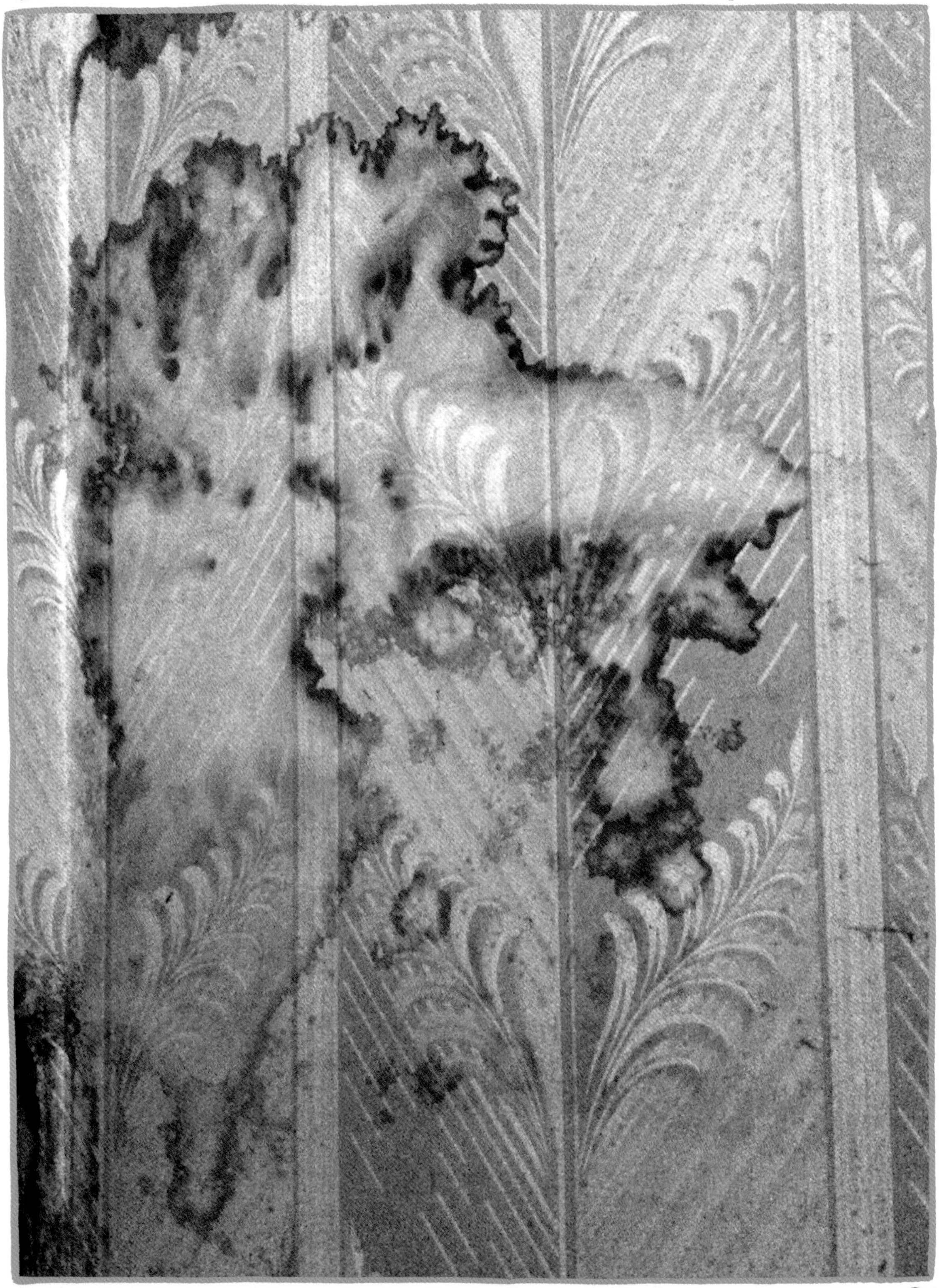

SEE THE EYES? SEE THE TEETH? ISN'T IT AMAZING?! THIS IMAGE MIRACULOUSLY APPEARED ON THE WALLPAPER IN THE HOME OF THE AUTHOR'S MOTHER.

THE AUTHOR:

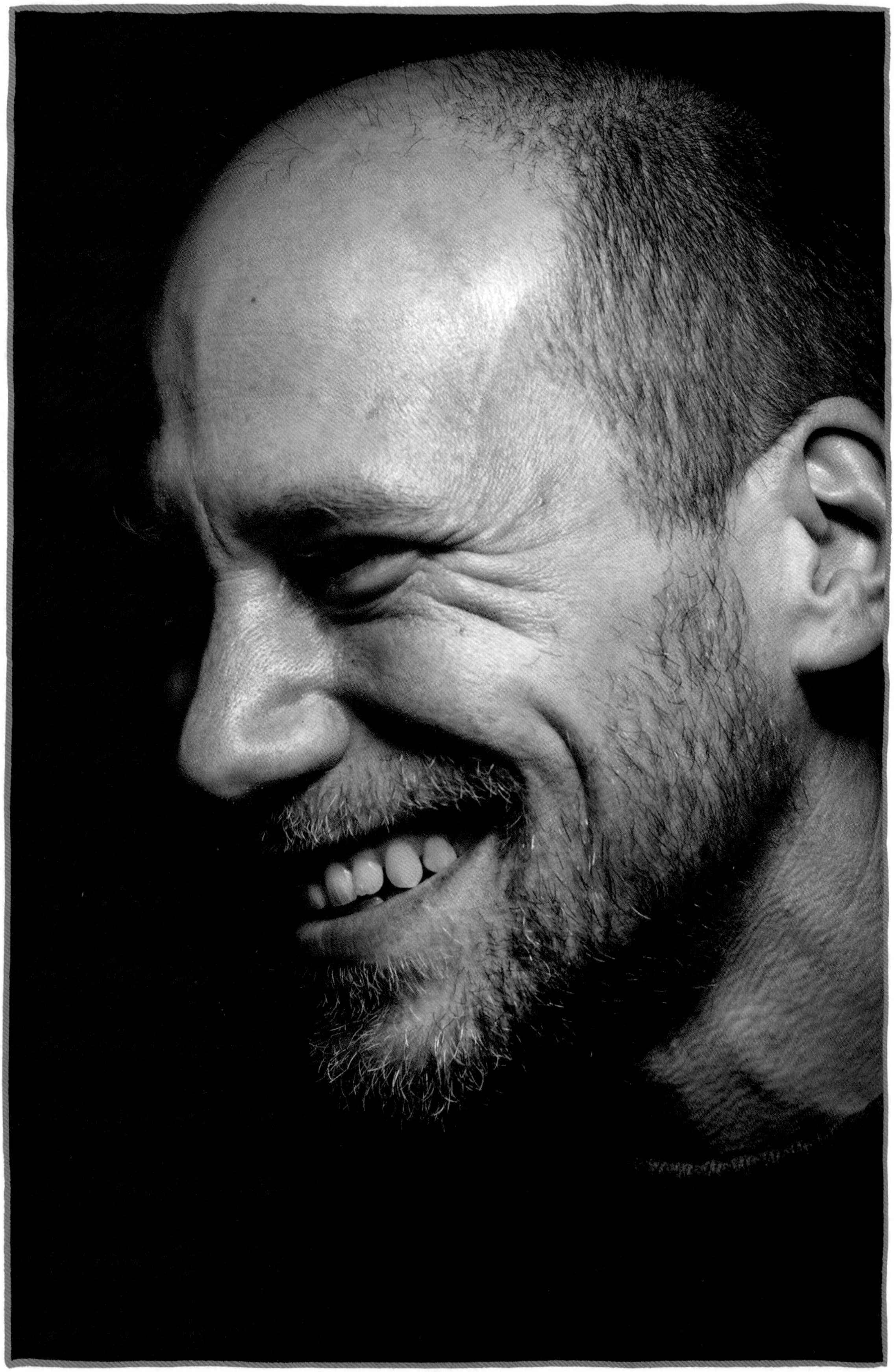

PHOTO BY SAM SIMON